## "You have ... tell me what to do!"

With a supreme effort, Lacey pushed and twisted out of his hold. "I'll shout if I want to," Lacey continued. "And if you don't like it you can leave!"

"We've been through that before," Cole retorted.

"Yes, we have." Her chin quivered. "And you'll be glad to know you've finally won. I'm leaving! The house is yours! Isn't that what you want?"

His expression hardened. "Yes," he snapped. "That's exactly what I want!" His heavy, angry strides carried him away and Lacey heard the door slam.

She didn't cry as she packed to leave. There didn't seem to be any tears inside her. She was just a big empty ache.

## JANET DAILEY AMERICANA

# TIDEWATER LOVER

**Harlequin Books**

TORONTO • NEW YORK • LONDON
AMSTERDAM • PARIS • SYDNEY • HAMBURG
STOCKHOLM • ATHENS • TOKYO • MILAN
MADRID • WARSAW • BUDAPEST • AUCKLAND

The state flower depicted on the cover of this book is dogwood.

Janet Dailey Americana edition published April 1988
Second printing November 1988
Third printing November 1989
Fourth printing November 1990
Fifth printing January 1992
Sixth printing October 1992
Seventh printing December 1992

ISBN 0-373-89896-7

Harlequin Presents edition published June 1979
Second printing February 1982

Original hardcover edition published in 1978
by Mills & Boon Limited

TIDEWATER LOVER

Printed in U.S.A.

# CHAPTER ONE

THE RING of the telephone checked the step Lacey Andrews had taken away from her desk. The light was blinking on the interoffice line. Shifting the stack of file folders to her left arm, Lacey reached across the desk to answer it. The movement swung her silky brown hair forward. She tucked it behind her right ear before lifting the receiver to the same ear.

"Lacey speaking," she identified herself automatically.

"You have a call from a Margo Richards on line three," was the reply.

A dark eyebrow flicked upward in surprise at her cousin's name. "Thanks, Jane." And Lacey pressed the plastic button of the third line, wondering with faint cynicism why Margo was phoning her. "Hello, Margo." Her brown eyes glanced toward the ceiling. Lacey knew this would not be a short conversation. Her cousin could spend an hour just saying what time it was.

"I'm sorry to call you at work, Lacey," the melodic voice rushed on, hardly a trace of sincere apology in her tone. "I don't mean to get you into any trouble with your boss, but I simply couldn't wait until tonight to talk to you."

"You aren't getting me into trouble. There are no

restrictions against receiving personal calls," Lacey explained with amused patience. "What is it that's so urgent?"

"I wanted to let you know that Bob and I are leaving tomorrow to fly to Florida to visit his parents. From there we'll be taking a two-week cruise in the Caribbean."

"Sounds marvelous!" Not for anything would Lacey permit even the tiniest suggestion of envy to creep into her voice. She adjusted a box pleat on her plaid skirt and settled down for a long dissertation from her cousin.

"It is exciting, isn't it?" Margo gushed. "It all happened so quickly, too. I mentioned in passing to Bob how romantic a cruise like that would be—and you know how Bob is. If I liked the moon, he'd try to buy it."

*Poor man*, Lacey thought. She hoped he would learn to say no to Margo before she spent all his money. Lacey was certain that Margo truly loved Bob, but she doubted if her love would ever mature as long as her slightest whim was indulged as if she were still a child.

"I've been dashing around madly ever since he told me," Margo continued. "Half of my summer wardrobe was so sadly dated that I would have been embarrassed if I'd worn it. Oh, Lacey, I wish you could see this gorgeous gown I bought! It's so daring I don't know if Bob will let me wear it. And there's this stunning pair of satin evening pajamas in a shimmering blue that's pos—"

"Margo, I'd love to hear all about your new clothes," Lacey interrupted, knowing that if she didn't stop her cousin now, she wouldn't. Margo's conversation was threatening to run longer than normal. Next she would be hearing the entertainment schedule of the cruise ship. A strong sense of loyalty to her job demanded that Lacey not spend an hour on a private phone call. "But I'm fairly busy at the moment. Maybe you should call me tonight."

"But that's just it. Bob and I are invited to a dinner party tonight—that's why I'm calling you now." There was an incredulous note in Margo's voice, as if she couldn't understand why Lacey was so stupid as not to have reasoned it out by herself.

Lacey gritted her teeth and smiled rigidly at the receiver. "Well, I really appreciate your letting me know you're going to be leaving." What else could she say?

"Oh, but that isn't why I called. I thought I told you." Lacey could imagine Margo's wide-eyed look of innocence.

"No, Margo, you didn't," she replied, concealing an impatient sigh. "Exactly why have you phoned?"

"I ran into Sally Drummond yesterday. Quite by accident," Margo assured her as she identified a close friend of Lacey's. "I was on my way to the car with an armful of packages when she came out of a restaurant."

Lacey sat down on the edge of her desk. She had absolutely no idea what Sally had to do with this phone call, but she would learn. There was simply no way to speed up Margo's explanation. It was an irritating fact, but unchangeable.

"I stopped to say hello," Margo went on. "Then we got to gossiping a bit—you know how that goes. Anyway, one subject led to another until finally we were talking about you."

"Really?" Lacey murmured dryly.

"Nothing bad or anything like that," Margo laughed. "Sally mentioned that you were going on vacation next week for two weeks, but she wasn't sure if you'd made any specific plans. Is that right?"

"Yes," Lacey admitted grudgingly. Her little excursions would pale in comparison to Margo's cruise.

"You aren't going away anywhere?"

"I thought I'd spend a couple of days with the folks, but outside of that, I'm just going to relax and do nothing."

"That's great!" Margo declared enthusiastically.

Lacey didn't think she would go as far as to say that, but it would be a refreshing change from the hectic pace of the office. Still, it was doubtful if Margo had had that reasoning in mind when she made her comment.

The truth was Lacey couldn't afford to leave the Tidewater area of Virginia to go anywhere on her vacation. A variety of unforeseen expenses, the largest being some major repairs to her car, had drained Lacey's savings account almost dry, but she was too proud to volunteer that information to her cousin.

"Why do you ask?" She tried to hurry Margo to the point of this conversation.

"I've been worried about our house and all our beautiful things," Margo stated. "Situated the way we are on the beach, virtually isolated from any close neighbors, you just never know what might happen. Especially with all the summer tourists that are showing up now. Someone could break into the house and steal everything we have the instant they noticed it was vacant. I've been in an absolute quandary as to what to do about it. You know what beautiful things we have, Lacey."

"Yes," Lacey agreed. Over a month ago Margo had taken her on a tour of the place, to show off—no other term could fit more perfectly—her home. She hated to admit to being envious, but she had fallen in love with her cousin's home.

"I was sitting here this morning, worrying myself half sick with what might happen while Bob and I are on the ship. Then I remembered Sally telling me that you were going on vacation and I knew I had the perfect solution. You could babysit the house while we're gone!"

Lacey hesitated. "I suppose. . . I could."

As she ran the idea over in her mind, it sounded like the perfect plan. A vacation spent in luxurious surroundings with the ocean and beach at her doorstep. It was something she wouldn't have been able to afford at twice her salary.

"I just knew you'd help me out!" Margo exclaimed.

"It will be my pleasure," Lacey returned sincerely, already picturing lazy days in the sun. Maybe she would even splurge on a new swimsuit.

"There is one thing," Margo paused. "I told you we were leaving tomorrow. Well, I just hate the thought of the house being empty for an hour. Could you. . . would you stay here tomorrow night?"

Breathing in deeply, Lacey wondered if her cousin knew what she was asking. Commuting from Virginia Beach to Newport News during rush hour traffic would practically mean rising with the sun. But tomorrow was Thursday. If she could arrange to have Saturday morning off, it would mean only having to make the round trip once.

"Sure," Lacey agreed finally. "I'll pack and drive out after work tomorrow."

"I'll be eternally grateful for this," Margo vowed effusively. "Now there's plenty of food, et cetera, in the house and I'll leave the front door key in the flowerpot near the door."

"Okay."

"You just make yourself at home, Lacey. Listen, I really have to run—I still have oodles of packing to do. See you when we get back from the Caribbean. Bye!"

"Bye." But Lacey's response was given to the dial tone buzzing in her ear.

Shrugging, she replaced the receiver on its cradle. It was typical of Margo. Once her objective was achieved she lost interest. But Lacey didn't bear any grudge. Thanks to Margo, her two weeks' vacation had suddenly taken on a new perspective.

Of course, she still had to talk to Mike Bowman, her employer, about Saturday morning. Straightening from the desk, Lacey walked to the twin set of metal cabinets in her office and deposited the folders on top. As she opened a drawer to begin the filing, the door to her office opened and Mike Bowman, who was one of the chief engineers for the construction company, walked in.

"Hello, Lacey," he greeted her absently, frowning as he paused beside her desk to go through the stack of messages waiting for him.

Brushing aside the sleek brown hair that curved across one side of her forehead, Lacey studied him for an instant. Mike was in his late thirties, a peppering of gray showing up in his dark hair; a confirmed bachelor—so he claimed.

Even with her limited experience, Lacey knew she could search a long time and never find an easier person to work for, nor one more fun on a date. They had dated occasionally in the last few months, although neither had spread the fact around to the others in the office. Mike was good-looking in a strong, dependable kind of way.

"Judging by your expression, I won't ask how your meeting went," Lacey offered with a sympathetic gleam in her brown eyes.

"Please don't." The corners of his mouth were pulled grimly down. "It was an exercise in frustration trying to explain to the big bosses the combination of circumstances that's put the Whitfield project so far behind schedule. Sometimes I think if they'd get out of their offices and out on the job sites, they might get a better understanding of what I'm up against."

"Maybe you should have suggested that," Lacey smiled.

"No, it's not their job." Mike sighed heavily in resignation. "They don't want to hear excuses, they want solutions. And they're right. I have to start coming up with solutions before the problems I have create more problems in and of themselves."

"Speaking of problems, I don't know if you remember or not, but my vacation starts next week."

"Don't remind me of that," Mike grimaced. "I don't want to remember it until Monday morning."

"Sorry, but I was hoping you might give me Saturday

morning off." There was a flash of even white teeth as Lacey smiled sympathetically.

"Why? I thought you said you weren't going anywhere on your vacation." He frowned, his hazel eyes confused as he met her gaze.

"My plans have changed slightly," she acknowledged. "My cousin called to ask me if I'd stay at her house in Virginia Beach while she and her husband are away on an impromptu vacation. They leave tomorrow, which means I'll move in tomorrow night. I'll have to commute on Friday—and Saturday, as well, unless you let me have the day off."

"Why not?" Mike shrugged.

"Thanks. I'll work late for you Friday to make up for it," Lacey promised.

"You'd better get out of this madhouse at five on the dot Friday or I might change my mind and postpone your vacation," he declared in a mock threat. "Then your cousin or whoever it was would have to find some other house-sitter. By the way, who's going to take your place here?"

"Donna is." Lacey knew the reaction that announcement would produce. Donna was not one of Mike's favorite people.

There was a skeptical glint in his eye at the name of Lacey's replacement. "You'd better leave the address and phone number of your cousin's house with Jane, just in case 'dumb Donna' gets things all loused up here or discovers she can't find something. Where did you say you'd be? Virginia Beach?"

"Yes. The house is right on the ocean. And so help me, Mike, if you call me to work on my vacation, I'll—"

Lacey never got a chance to finish her warning vow.

"On the beach, you say? Hell," he chuckled, "I just might take my vacation and join you. It sounds like paradise. You know what the travel brochures say—Virginia is for lovers. Maybe we should both take the next two weeks to prove they're right. I could stand to get away from the office myself." Both of them knew he was only dreaming. There wasn't a chance of Mike's having any time off.

"If you aren't doing anything Sunday, why don't you come over?" she suggested, knowing it was wishful thinking Mike was indulging in, but extending the invitation as consolation.

"It's a date," Mike replied without any hesitation, settling for a day instead of two weeks. "I'll bring a couple of steaks and we'll cook outside."

"Terrific," Lacey agreed.

The interoffice line rang and Lacey walked to her desk to answer it. Jane, the receptionist, responded immediately, "Didn't I see Mr. Bowman come in, Lacey?"

"Yes."

"Good. Mr. Whitfield is on line one. He's called a half a dozen times." She didn't bother to add that by this time Mr. Whitfield was a very impatient man. The tone of her voice was riddled with the statement.

"Thanks, Jane." Lacey replaced the receiver and glanced hesitantly at Mike. "Whitfield is on line one," she informed him.

He bared his teeth in a grimace. "I've just been through one frustrating series of explanations. See if you can use that soothing voice of yours and put him off for a while."

Sitting down in her chair, Lacey accepted the challenge. After all, in a sense it was part of her job to shield Mike from unwanted phone calls. Mike stood expectantly beside her desk, watching her intently as she picked up the phone and pushed the button for the first line.

"Mr. Bowman's office. May I help you?" she inquired in her most pleasant manner.

"Yes," came the crisp male voice. "I would like to speak to Mr. Bowman."

It was a command, not a request, and Lacey could tell the difference. Still she persisted. "I'm terribly sorry, but Mr. Bowman is on another line at the moment. May I take a message, please?"

"He's on another line, is he?" There was no mistaking the sarcastic skepticism in the response.

"Yes. May I have him call you back when he's through?" Lacey offered.

"No, you may not!" the voice snapped in her ear. She flinched slightly at the coldly raised voice and held the receiver away from her ear. "No doubt Bowman is standing beside you to see if you're going to succeed in stalling me off. But I assure you, miss, that you will not."

Whether it was the accuracy of his accusation or her temper reacting to his acid tone, Lacey didn't know, but she abandoned her attempt to be pleasant, resorting to the sarcasm he had used.

"I assure you, Mr. Whitfield, that Mr. Bowman is on another line. However, since your call seems to be so urgent that you feel the necessity to be rude, I shall see if I can interrupt him. Please hold the line." Without giving him a chance to respond, she pushed the hold button, shutting him off. Fiery lights burned in her brown eyes as she glanced at Mike, anger in the tight-lipped line of her mouth.

"I'm sorry I asked you to speak to him, Lacey," Mike said immediately. "I'll take the call in my office."

"I wish you could tell him to go take a flying leap into a dry lake," she fumed.

"Believe me, it's a temptation," he sighed. "But it is his time and money I'm spending every day that project falls further behind schedule. He has a right to know what's going on."

"He doesn't have any right to be such a...a...."

"Careful," Mike warned with a teasing wink. "Ladies aren't supposed to use the word you're searching for!"

"I don't feel very much like a lady at this moment," Lacey muttered, glaring at the blinking light that indicated that Mr. Whitfield was still holding.

"Just think about the two weeks you're going to spend away from all this," Mike suggested in an attempt to calm her anger as he started toward his private office.

As quickly as her temper had flared, it died. "And I'll occasionally spend a moment or two feeling sorry for you back at the office slogging away while I bask on the sand," laughed Lacey.

Minutes after Mike had entered his office, the light stopped blinking and held steady. Lacey felt sorry for him. Considering the vituperative mood Whitfield was in, it wouldn't be easy for Mike to explain about the new delays on Whitfield's construction project. He was in for a tongue-lashing, but she knew Mike would handle the unpleasant situation in his usual calm way.

With a sigh, Lacey walked back to the metal cabinets to resume her filing of the folders she had placed on top. The door to her office opened. Lacey glanced over her shoulder and smiled as she recognized the girl who had entered.

"Hi, Maryann," she greeted the girl who was one of her best friends. "What are you doing?" It was purely a rhetorical question.

"I am escaping," Maryann Carver declared and sank into the spare, straight-backed chair at Lacey's desk. She had the air of a person who had been pushed to the limit. "A word of advice, Lacey. Don't ever take a job as a payroll clerk. No, two words of advice," she corrected herself. "Don't ever put off going to the dentist."

"Is your tooth bothering you again?" Lacey sympathized.

"Yes. Have you got any aspirin for a suffering fool? I forgot to bring any with me this morning and this tooth is killing me." Maryann combed her fingers through hair that couldn't make up its mind whether it was brown or blond.

"I think there is a bottle of aspirin in the middle drawer of my desk. Help yourself." Lacey slipped a folder into its proper place in the file. "You really should see a dentist."

"I am, at four this afternoon. All I have to do is survive till then." The desk drawer was opened and pills rattled in their plastic bottle. "He's only going to fix this one tooth. I have to go back in a couple of weeks for a regular checkup. You know, that's one good thing about mothers. They always make sure you have your regular checkups when you live at home. Of course, I'll never tell my mother there are advantages to living at home. She'd have me back in my old room before I could say no."

"So would my mother." Lacey closed the file drawer and returned to her desk, that task finished.

"Hey, I just remembered!" With pills in her hand, Maryann paused on her way to the water cooler. "You start your vacation on Monday. Are you still planning to visit your parents in Richmond?"

"Just for a weekend. My cousin Margo called a few minutes ago. She's going off on a cruise with her husband and asked me to stay in their beach house while they are away."

"Beach house? How lucky can you get? Are you staying there by yourself? Or would you like a roommate?"

"But that roommate—" Lacey knew Maryann was suggesting herself "—would have to commute back and forth to work every day."

Maryann grimaced. "You only brought that up because you want the place to yourself."

Lacey smiled away the remark. "It's certainly going to be a better vacation than I had planned. Imagine, two weeks with the ocean at my doorstep and an uncrowded beach." Each time she thought about it, it sounded more idyllic. As she set the bottle of aspirin back into the middle drawer, Lacey noticed the light had gone off on the first line of the telephone. "Poor Mike. I wonder if he needs an aspirin."

"Why should he? Don't tell me he has a toothache,

too?'' Maryann filled a paper cup with water and downed the aspirin in her hand.

"No, but I bet he has a headache." Lacey motioned toward the telephone. "He just finished talking to the sarcastic Mr. Whitfield. That man is the cause of many a headache."

"Who is Mr. Whitfield?"

"A very rude and obnoxious person. Doubly so because the complex we're building for him is way behind schedule. He's a real pain. I wish Mike would punch him in the mouth some day. After the job is done, of course," she added.

"Tut, tut, Lacey. The customer is always right." There was a definite twinkle of laughter in Maryann's eyes. "Look, I'd love to sit and exchange miseries all day, but we both have a lot of work to do. We'll have lunch tomorrow and you can tell me all about the beach house and your sarcastic Mr. Whitfield. I suppose the house is fabulous and I'll be green with envy. You'll leave when? Sunday?"

"No, tomorrow night. I'll have to commute on Friday, but Mike gave me Saturday off."

"Lucky you," Maryann sighed. "I wish I had him to work for instead of that crochety old pruneface."

Lacey merely laughed. "Hope your tooth gets better," she offered in goodbye as her friend opened the outer door.

"So do I. See you tomorrow."

ON THURSDAY EVENING, with her small hatchback loaded with suitcases and odds and ends, Lacey drove into the driveway of Margo Richards's home. Her brown eyes roved over the elegantly simple lines of the beach house, painted a cream white that matched the foamy whitecaps of the ocean breaking beyond the dunes.

Only a fool would deny that she was looking forward to having the beautiful home all to herself for the next two weeks, and Lacey was not a fool. A faint smile curved her lips, which bore little traces of strawberry gloss.

Grabbing her cosmetic case and one of the smaller pieces of luggage from the rear seat of the car, Lacey stepped out and walked buoyantly to the front door. Intent on reaching the flowerpot where Margo had said she would leave the key, Lacey didn't pay attention to what was beneath her feet.

The toe of her sandal hooked the roughly textured mat in front of the door, catapulting her forward. The cosmetic case flew from her hand, the lock failing to hold so that the lid snapped open to scatter her cosmetics onto the concrete slab. Fortunately Lacey managed to regain her balance a stumbling second before she joined the case.

"Why don't you pay attention to where you're going, Lacey?" she scolded herself, then stooped to pick up the items scattered before her.

A gleam of metal winked at her near the edge of the mat. Curious, she reached for it, pushing the mat aside to reveal a shiny key. She studied it for a second, then tried in in the door lock. It opened with the first attempt.

"How typical of Margo," she murmured aloud, leaving the door open while she refastened her cosmetic case. "She forgot where she told me she'd put the key and chose the most likely place."

Inside the entrance foyer of the two-story house, Lacey paused. From her previous single visit to the house, she remembered that the rooms on the ground floor consisted of a study, a rec room and a utility room. The rest was taken up by a garage.

The main living area of the house was at the top of the stairs to her left. Looking up the staircase, Lacey admired again the tall built-in cabinet stretching from the landing of the open stairwell to the ceiling of the top floor. The carved moldings of its white-painted wood were etched with a darkly brilliant blue. Through the panes of glass in its tall doors, assorted vases and figurines of complementing blues were deftly scattered among a collection of books.

With cosmetic case and suitcase in hand, Lacey mounted the steps. A large potted tree stood near the white railing at the head of the steps. All was silent. The click of her shoes on the hardwood floor of the second story sounded loud to her own ears, but she resisted the impulse to tiptoe.

The decor of the stairwell was an introduction to the white and blue world of the living room. Matching cream white sofas with throw pillows of peacock blue occupied the large area rug, predominantly patterned in blue, in front of the white brick fireplace. Again, the assorted statues and figurines carried the theme of blue, accented by the hanging plants and potted plants that abounded in the room.

The dining room and kitchen were an extension of the living room with no walls to divide them. A mixture of white rattan and white wicker furniture in the dining room added an informal touch, with the emphasis subtly changing from blue to green, mostly by the usage of plants.

Setting her cases down, Lacey walked to the large picture windows fronting the ocean. The blue drapes were pulled open to reveal an expansive view of the sea and the beckoning sandy beach. She turned away. There was time enough to explore the outdoors later.

An investigation of the kitchen with its countered bar to the dining room indicated that there was an ample supply of canned goods on hand and three or four days' worth of food in the refrigerator. She would fix her evening meal later. First on the agenda was to unpack and get settled in.

The bedrooms branched off the hallway to the left of the living room. Lacey only glanced into the master bedroom. The two guest rooms were smaller but still comfortably large. She chose the one with a view of the ocean. The guest rooms shared a bath that had its entrance from the hall.

Pastel yellow joined with the predominant theme of blue in the room's decor, giving a cheery impression of sunshine and ocean. Lacey glanced admiringly at the furnishings before catching her reflection in the mirror.

"I could grow to like this style of living." She winked at the mirror. The dark-eyed girl in the mirror, her seal-brown hair styled in a boyish cut that made her look ultrafeminine, winked back.

An hour later she had brought in all her luggage from the car, which she had parked inside the garage. A few of Margo's winter clothes were in the closet, but there was still plenty of room for Lacey's belongings. Fixing a plate of cheese, cold meat and fruit, she ate alone at the dining table, facing the ocean. She lingered there, listening to the symphony of the surf, gentle waves breaking on the sandy beach. The music of the ocean was soothing and she hated to leave it, but there were other things to be done.

The picture-perfect house seemed to demand tidiness. Lacey washed the few dishes and put them away, effectively eradicating any trace of her presence. Then, and only then, did she submit to the call of the sea and the beckoning of the empty stretch of sand she could see from the windows.

The setting sun was turning the sand into molten gold when she finally retraced her steps to the house, tired yet oddly refreshed by the salt air. After showering and setting the alarm, she crawled into bed, falling asleep almost as soon as her head touched the pillow.

She stirred once in the night, waking long enough to identify her surroundings before slipping immediately back into a sound sleep. The infuriating buzz of the alarm wakened her as the morning sun was crowning the ocean's horizon. Her groping hand found the shut-off knob and quickly silenced it.

The long drive ahead of her in the morning traffic made her groan, "I'm glad I only have to do this once!"

Stumbling out of bed, she walked bleary-eyed into the kitchen, wearing only her long silky pajamas. A pitcher of orange juice was in the refrigerator. Filling a glass from the cupboard, she downed the wake-up juice quickly before putting water on to boil for instant coffee.

She wasted little time in the bathroom with washing and applying the little makeup she used. Back in her bedroom, she donned a plaid skirt and matching satiny textured blouse in mint green. Her return to the kitchen coincided with the first rising bubbles of the water.

With a cup of instant coffee in her hand, Lacey stifled a yawn and walked to the glass-paned door in the dining room. It led to the balcony overlooking the ocean. The breeze blowing from the sea was brisk and invigorating—exactly what she needed to chase the cobwebs of sleep from her head.

Leaning against a rail, she watched the incoming tide, mesmerized by the waves rushing one after another in to shore. For a while she lost all track of time, sipping at the steaming coffee until the cup was drained.

The sound of a car engine broke the spell of the waves, and she turned with a frown. The ocean breeze made it difficult to tell where the sound was coming from, but it seemed very near. Probably an early-morning fisherman, she decided and reentered the house.

In the kitchen, she started to rinse her cup and spoon under the tap. Her dark eyes rounded in surprise at the orange juice glass sitting on the counter.

"You're losing your grip, gal," she mocked herself as she picked up the dirtied glass. "These early-morning hours must be affecting your memory. You obviously didn't wash the glass as you thought you had."

Quickly wiping the cup, glass and spoon, she put them in their proper places in the cupboards. A glance at her watch told her she was running behind schedule. She quickly gathered her purse from the bedroom and sped down the stairs to the garage and her car.

The morning traffic through Norfolk was as heavy as

she had thought it would be at that hour. And the congestion at the tunnel under the ship channel to Hampton Road and Newport News lost her a lot of time. She arrived at the office twenty minutes late and spent all morning trying to make up for the lost time.

Coming back from her lunch break at a crowded café, which was hardly guaranteed to aid the digestion nor calm the nerves, Lacey stopped by the receptionist. One look at Jane's flustered and anxious expression told her that office gossip was not on the girl's mind.

"That Mr. Whitfield is calling again, Lacey. And he's very upset," Jane burst out. "I told him to call back at one-thirty. I thought Mr. Bowman would be back in his office by then, but he just called to say he was tied up at another job site. Mr. Whitfield is going to be furious when he finds out Mr. Bowman isn't here."

Lacey's first impulse was to say "Tough!" But she had felt the steel edge of Mr. Whitfield's tongue before and knew why Jane dreaded his call. Using a smile to hide her gritted teeth, she said, "Put the call from Mr. Whitfield through to me. I'll explain."

She was barely seated behind her desk, her bag stowed in one of the lower drawers, when the interoffice line buzzed. It was Jane, relaying the message that Mr. Whitfield was holding on line two. Lacey murmured a wry thanks at the message.

"Don't lose your temper," she cautioned herself with a personal pep talk. "Stay calm and pleasant regardless of what he says. Don't do anything that would make matters worse for Mike."

The advice was excellent, she knew, but just before she took the call she stuck her tongue out at the blinking light. It was a true expression of her feelings at the moment, combined with relief that tomorrow she would be away from Mr. Whitfield and the office for two glorious weeks.

"Mr. Bowman's office." When she spoke there was enough honey in her voice to fill a hive.

"Put me through to Bowman." Impatience crackled in the male voice.

"I'm sorry, but Mr. Bowman isn't in. I don't expect him until later this afternoon. May I help you?" Lacey kept the saccharine quality in her words and waited for the explosion. It came.

"I was told—" he began with cold anger.

"Yes, I know what you were told, Mr. Whitfield," she interrupted sweetly. "He was expected back at one-thirty, but he was unavoidably detained at one of the job sites."

"So you're claiming that he's not there?" came the taunt.

"I am not claiming it. I am stating it." It was a delight to hear the smiling confidence in her own voice.

"I don't know at which job site Bowman is, but I can assure you, Miss—"

"—Andrews," Lacey supplied.

"—Miss Andrews, that it isn't mine. Yesterday Bowman promised me a full complement of trades. I've been to the job site, Miss Andrews—" his rich voice was ominously low and freezing in its anger "—and a skeleton could rattle through the building and not find anyone to scare. You tell Bowman when he gets back to his office that I expect to hear from him—immediately!"

If, as Jane had indicated, there were problems on one

of the other job sites, Mike would not be in any mood to contact Mr. Whitfield when he returned. Taking a deep breath, Lacey plunged into her mission of mercy. It was the least she could do after Mike had given her Saturday morning off.

"I'm familiar with your project, Mr. Whitfield," she volunteered, "and the circumstances that have interfered with its completion. Perhaps I could explain."

"You?" The taunt was not so much skepticism as it was mocking contempt.

Lacey bristled, but steadfastly refused to take the bait of replying in kind. "Yes, Mr. Whitfield, me. I'm aware of what's happening on the various projects, including yours."

"Which is precisely nothing."

"For a very good reason," Lacey insisted, her composure cracking for an instant.

"All right." He accepted her offer to explain with a decided challenge. "Tell me why there aren't any painters on the job?"

"The painters aren't there because the bulk of the work left for them is in the various washrooms, work that they can't do until the tile setters are finished. The tile setters aren't there because the plumber isn't finished. You see, Mr. Whitfield, it's a vicious circle."

"Why aren't the plumbers on the job?" he demanded diffidently. "The story you've just told me isn't new, Miss Andrews. I've heard it all from Bowman, along with a promise that the plumbers would be out there today without fail."

"At the time that Mr. Bowman told you that, he fully believed it would happen. The problem is that the shipment of bathroom fixtures hasn't arrived. Yesterday the plumber misinformed him that it had come in. Late this morning, Mi—Mr. Bowman found out differently. I know he regrets the delay as much as you do," Lacey added with honey-coated politeness.

But Whitfield completely ignored the last comment. "Where is the shipment of fixtures?"

"I don't know, sir. I do know they were shipped several weeks ago from the manufacturer, but they haven't arrived."

"In other words, they're lost en route and you're saying, 'Too bad,' " he jeered.

"Of course not," Lacey protested.

"Then what freight company were they shipped by?"

"I . . . I don't know."

"What about the manifest numbers, points of origin? Do you know any of that, Miss Andrews?" Whitfield continued his biting questions.

"No, I don't." She was becoming flustered, color warming her cheeks.

"Do you know if anyone has put a tracer on the shipment?"

"No, I don't know if it's been done," she admitted stiffly.

"Has Bowman or the plumbing contractor looked into alternate suppliers for the fixtures, or are they intending to wait for the day when they show up?" he snapped.

"I'm sure they don't intend to—"

"I damned well hope not!"

"Really, Mr. Whitfield." Her lips were compressed in a tight line. "I—"

"Really, Miss Andrews," he interrupted caustically, "it seems to me if human skill and persistence can put a man on the moon, then it should also be possible to find a lost shipment of toilets, don't you think?"

"Yes, of course—"

"Then may I suggest that since you are supposed to be a secretary, you should use your time to see what can be done about finding the shipment!" And the line went dead.

Lacey sputtered uselessly into the mouthpiece before slamming the receiver on its cradle. His clear-thinking logic made her feel like a bumbling idiot.

A tracer should have been put out on the shipment several days ago, but it galled that Whitfield had been the one to point out the oversight. Picking up the telephone again, Lacey made the first step to rectify the mistake.

# CHAPTER TWO

IT WAS CRAZY, Lacey acknowledged to herself as she stretched lazily like a cat. Here it was a mild summer night and she had all the windows open and a fire burning in the fireplace. But it seemed to somehow fit her mood, with the breeze off the ocean carrying a tangy salt scent; the gentle sound of the breakers rushing in to the beach; and the crackling of flames dancing to the soft music on the stereo.

After the hectic last day at the office, with the irritating phone call from that Whitfield man, and the long drive through evening traffic to Margo's house, Lacey had virtually collapsed on Friday night, sleeping until nearly noon this morning. An afternoon swim had been the only exertion she had allowed herself, outside of cooking a high-calorie Italian dinner all for herself.

Now, with the moonlight silvering the ocean and the yellow flames lighting the blackened hearth, Lacey's sole desire was to curl up on the sofa and read. Kicking off her gold mules, she carried out her wish.

The filmy baby-doll pajamas were decidedly brief, she realized as she tucked her legs beneath her, but she shrugged unconcernedly. There weren't any neighbors close by and a peeping Tom would have to be a giant to see in the second-story windows. Here in the flat country of Virginia's Tidewater basin along the coast, there wasn't such a thing as a hill or a mountain.

The blue-bottomèd lamp beside the sofa cast a small pool of light on the pages of the book in Lacey's hand. Reclining against the fluffy pillows, she found her place and began reading. Soon her head began nodding lethargically until finally the book slipped from her fingers and she dozed.

An hour later something wakened her. Tiredly she glanced around, deciding it had been a log cracking in the fireplace. Closing the book, she set it on the chrome and white stand beside the lamp and switched off the light.

As sleepy as she was, she knew she should go to bed, but it was so pleasant and comfortable in front of the fire. Snuggling deeper into the pillows, she gazed at the yellow flames licking the nearly disintegrated wood in the fireplace.

From the bottom of the entrance stairs she heard the rattle of the doorknob, and the remnants of sleep fled as every nerve screamed in alertness. Some burglar was breaking in! And she was there all alone with no neighbors near enough to hear her cries.

Her bare feet didn't make a sound on the patterned rug as she darted to the telephone beside the other sofa. But the line was dead when she picked up the receiver. Panic raced through her veins.

It was too late to run. The front door had already been opened and there was the quiet even tread of footsteps on the stairs. Instinct sent Lacey racing madly to the fireplace. There was a brief clang of metal against metal as she grabbed the poker from its rack.

The footsteps on the stairs paused for an instant and

she froze a foot or two in front of the fireplace. Both of her shaking hands were clutching the poker, holding it like a baseball bat in front of her.

The steps resumed their climb. With only the flickering, dying flames of the fire to provide light in the darkened house, the stairwell was encased in shadows. Yet from these shadows emerged a darker figure, halting immobile at the head of the steps.

Breathing became painful for Lacey. She swallowed, trying to ease the paralysis in her throat.

The figure moved nearer, into the half light cast by the fire. Dark trousers gave way to a lighter-colored top, a knit of some sort, Lacey guessed unconsciously, judging by the way it outlined the breadth of his chest and shoulders. The man's face was all angles and planes, the firelight casting more shadows than it revealed. Yet the rough contours of his face gave her the impression that he was regarding her with curious—if not amused—surprise.

He took another step nearer and her heart jumped into her throat, blocking any bravado words of challenge. The shadows dissipated and she found herself staring into a pair of blue eyes, dark as indigo.

They began to make a slow, assessing sweep of her, traveling down the long column of her throat, over the jutting curves of her breast, noticing the slimness of her waist and hips, and following the length of bare legs to her bare toes, then reversed the order.

Lacey wasn't aware that the firelight flickering behind her made the filmy pajamas virtually transparent. Her only sensation was the way his eyes seemed to burn through her, increasing her feelings of danger.

When the unnerving pair of blue eyes leisurely made their return to her face, they skimmed over the fine bones and the sophisticated short cut of her silky brown hair. Lacey trembled when his gaze finally ensnared hers, her knuckles whitening as she gripped the poker tighter.

"Bob told me I would find everything I want here, but I didn't realize he meant it literally," the intruder mused, his tone riddled with suggestion.

Lacey brandished the poker. "Get out of here!" Her voice was a croaking whisper, making a mockery out of her attempt to threaten him.

She heard his throaty chuckle and wanted to run, but her legs were trembling. She had never been so terrified in her life as she was at that moment. There were so many things that could happen to her and she was trying desperately not to visualize any of them.

"You'd better get out of here," she warned again, this time with a steadier voice, "or I'll. . . I'll call the police."

She glanced at the telephone, inching closer toward it. She knew it was dead, but she was taking the chance that he had nothing to do with it.

"Sorry—" there was laughter in his voice, rich and low "—but the telephone has been temporarily disconnected."

As she breathed in quickly in despair, a tiny sob of panic made itself heard. She saw the male contour of his mouth curve into a smile that was oddly gentle, if mockingly indulgent.

"Why don't you tell me who you are and what you're doing here?" he suggested.

His question struck her as being so absurd that she was speechless. It became obvious that her presence wasn't going to intimidate him into leaving. She would have to think of something else.

"I'm not here alone, you know," lied Lacey. "My husband has gone to the store and he'll be back any minute. You'd better leave before he comes."

"Is he now?" The intruder merely smiled. "That's good. Maybe when he gets here, you'll put down that poker and start explaining a few things."

He took another step forward and Lacey raised the poker to strike. Her heart was hammering against her ribs, her stomach churning with fear.

"Don't come any closer," she threatened shakily, "or I'll bash your head in!"

He stopped, the lazy smile still curving his mouth. His stance was indolent, but Lacey wasn't deceived. There wasn't any spare flesh on his muscular frame and a man that physically fit could react in a split second, like a predatory animal.

"I believe you would try," he acknowledged, but in his acknowledgment he was implying that she would be no match for him even with the poker.

Behind Lacey a log in the fireplace popped loudly. The explosive sound startled her to the point that, for a scant second, she thought she was being attacked from the rear.

Before she could assimilate that the sound had been caused by the innocuous popping of a burning log, the steel teeth of a trap had closed around her right wrist, the hand with the major responsibility of holding the poker.

A strangled "No!" was torn from her throat as the weapon was ripped from her grasp.

Adrenalin surged through her system. Where once her limbs had been shaky and weak with fright, they now throbbed with new strength. She struck out at her attacker, arms and legs flailing at anything solid. And there was a great deal that was solid.

At first he was satisfied to merely hold her arm and ward off the bulk of her blows, but as her accuracy improved, he changed his tactics. Lacey felt herself being bodily twisted onto the sofa. Primitive alarm raced through her frantic heartbeats when she felt the force of his weight following to press her against the cushions.

With panicked breaths, she strained to rid herself of the crushing weight of his chest—to no avail. His sheer maleness was awakening all sorts of danger signals and she reacted all the more wildly. The bruising fingers pinning her shoulders to the sofa and thwarting the ineffectual hammering of her fists easily kept her his captive.

As she made a superhuman attempt to twist away, she felt the delicate strap of her pajama top tearing beneath his fingers. It was an inadvertent happening, but the touch of his hand against her now bare skin made her blood run cold with terror.

His body heat had already burned its male imprint on her. She heard him curse softly when she muffled a sob of fear by sinking her teeth into her lip. She detected a trace of liquor—Scotch—in the warm breath that fanned her cheek.

"Will you stop struggling?" he demanded roughly. "I don't want to hurt you."

His assertion flashed through her brain. Immediately Lacey recalled some professional advice she had either read or heard that suggested a woman should not do anything to incite an attacker into further violence.

Gradually she stopped fighting his hold, although her muscles remained tense, waiting for his next move and the slimmest chance of escape. Her breathing was labored and deep.

"That's better," he said in approval, and shifted to one side, easing the weight from on top of her while retaining a firm hold, as if knowing she would run at the first opportunity.

"Let me go!" Lacey flashed in a hoarse voice. She knew he wouldn't, but needed to make the demand so he would realize she wasn't totally submissive.

"Not yet."

In the dim light she caught the brief glimmer of white teeth and knew he was smiling—laughing at her. It stung that she was so helpless in the face of his superior strength.

He seemed to move toward her and she cringed into the cushions. But his arm reached above her head to switch on the lamp beside the sofa.

Lacey blinked warily in the blinding light, calming under the inspection by the dark blue eyes. She couldn't hold his gaze for long. It was too strangely disturbing, oddly making her feel guilty, and the sensation rattled her.

"Now for some explanations," he stated, eyeing her steadily. "What are you doing in this house?"

"I'm...I'm living here." Lacey frowned in confusion.

Doubt flickered sardonically in his narrowed gaze. "You own the house?" he queried.

"Well, no, not exactly." She wondered why his question made her feel so uncomfortable. She had a perfectly legitimate right to be in the house.

Her left hand was free and she raised it to brush a glistening brown strand of hair from the corner of her eye. His narrowed gaze followed the movement, as if anticipating that she might be intending to strike out at him again.

"Not exactly?" He repeated her phrase. In the blink of an eye, her left hand was caught by his. "And what about your husband? You said he'd be here any minute. Yet your ring finger is bare and there's no sign that you've ever worn a ring on that finger."

Lacey had been caught in her lie and she felt as guilty as she had when she was a child. "It becomes obvious that you weren't expecting your husband, despite your provocative garb."

His gaze flicked to the filmy yellow pajamas more or less covering her breasts, the torn strap resting in her cleavage. Lacey was hotly reminded of the little clothing she had on—and the firm outline of his male length beside her on the narrow sofa.

"I don't think," he continued, "you're expecting anyone."

"You can't be sure of that," she retorted.

"Can't I?" he countered smoothly. "Women invariably cake themselves with makeup and dab perfume in erotic places when they plan to entertain their lovers. Your face is scrubbed clean and—" he turned her left hand and lifted the inside of her wrist closer to his face, catching the clean fragrance of soap instead of expensive perfume "—you aren't wearing Chanel No. 5."

"So what!" Lacey jerked her hand away. "None of

this is any of your business and I don't have to explain to you. You're the one who broke into the house and accosted me. You...." She stopped short, realizing she shouldn't have reminded him of his reason for being there nor that she could easily identify him to the police.

The metallic glitter in his eyes reinforced the thought. "I broke into the house?" He repeated her words with a steely coldness that rang a familiar note in her memory, but Lacey was too caught up in the present to dwell on it. "You have an uncanny knack for telling tales."

"Telling tales...?" she began indignantly.

"Yes, tales." His hand moved. In the next instant he was holding a key in front of her face. "I used a key to get into the house. You are the one who broke in."

Lacey stared at it open-mouthed. "That's impossible!" she exclaimed finally. "Just because you say that's a key to the door, that doesn't mean it is."

"Believe me, it is." He smiled lazily, folding his fingers around the key and placing it back in his pocket. "So it's time for you to cut the innocent act."

"Act?"

He ignored her look of outrage. "You have two choices. Either get dressed and get out—I presume you do have some other clothes—or if you're desperately in need of a place to sleep tonight, I can recommend my bed." His finger traced the hollow of her collarbone, sending fiery tingles over her skin. "The last couple of nights I've found it to be quite comfortable, if slightly empty."

"The last couple of nights!" Lacey burst out angrily.

"I think this house has developed an echo," he chuckled.

"You accuse me of telling tales! You have to be the

absolute tops," she sputtered. "You're nothing but a liar! Trying to con me into thinking you have any right to be in this house. Well, you just got caught in your own snare. I'll have you know that I've been sleeping in this house for the last two nights, as well, and I certainly haven't seen you."

"You don't give up, do you?" he declared with an exasperated sigh, and swung his feet to the floor to stand up.

"No, I don't," Lacey retorted, her brown eyes snapping. "And since you've so magnanimously given me the choice of staying here with you or going, I'll leave!"

"Good." His mouth had thinned into a grim line. "And pass on the word to any of your friends who were thinking this house might be vacant and available for a few nights' free lodging that it isn't."

Lacey was on her feet, halfway across the living room headed toward her bedroom, when he finished his comment. She stopped, glaring at him over her shoulder.

"I'll pass the word along," she promised impulsively. "As soon as I'm dressed, I'm going to get into my car and drive straight to the police." Turning away, she muttered aloud, "Margo was right to worry about leaving this place empty while they were away."

Long strides cleaved the distance between them. The soft flesh of her arm was grabbed to spin her around. She clutched at the drooping side of her pajama top, feeling the inherent intimidation of his looming height. But she faced him boldly.

"What did you say just now?" he demanded.

"I said I was going straight to the police," she returned coolly.

"Not that." He frowned impatiently, not relaxing his biting hold of her arm. "The last part that you muttered under your breath."

"About Margo?" Lacey questioned with surprise.

His gaze sharpened. "Who's she?"

"The owner of the house, of course. Didn't you know that?" she asked sarcastically.

"I knew it," he answered, nodding. "I'm just wondering how you found out. I suppose you've been snooping around the house this evening."

Lacey counted to ten swiftly. "Margo Richards happens to be my cousin."

"Really?" he said with jeering skepticism.

"Yes, really." She forced a smile.

"Then where is your cousin now?"

"She and her husband flew to Florida to visit his family before leaving on a Caribbean cruise. That's why I'm here, so the house won't be standing vacant while they're gone," Lacey said with all of the righteousness of the wronged. "You're the trespasser, not I."

"And Margo asked you to stay here?" he repeated, drawing his head back to study her as he let go of her arm.

"Yes."

"Her husband Bob asked me to stay," he told her.

"What?" Lacey was taken aback for a minute by his statement, then she shrugged it away. "You don't honestly expect me to believe that."

"Believe it or not, it's the truth." He reached into the pocket of his khaki-colored top and took out a pack of cigarettes, calmly lighting one while Lacey stared at him with disbelief. "I don't know your cousin Margo very well—'' he blew a thin trail of smoke into the air ''—but Bob's family and mine have been friends for years.''

"Can you prove that?" she challenged. "Bob should be with his parents now. Why don't you call him?"

"I've already explained that the telephone is dead. They had their service interrupted while they're on vacation. That's the main reason I agreed to stay here—to get away from the telephone."

"Then you can't prove you know Bob," Lacey concluded.

He studied the glowing tip of his cigarette. "Do you know where they went on their honeymoon?"

"Yes," Lacey admitted, but she wasn't about to be trapped. "Do you?"

"To Hawaii. The first day there Bob stayed out in the sun too long and spent the next two days of their honeymoon in the hospital with sunstroke."

"He did ask you to stay in the house!" she exclaimed in a breathy voice.

"That's what I've been telling you."

"And you claim you've been staying here since Thursday night?" Lacey frowned.

"Not claim. I have been staying here—in the guest bedroom," he replied.

"But so have I." She ran her fingers through the thickness of her short hair. "Oh." Pieces of the puzzle started to fall into place. "Oh!" They began fitting together rapidly.

"Oh, my gosh," she whispered, and turned the full force of her brown gaze on him. "Did Bob give you the key to the front door in person?"

"No, he left it for me."

"Where? Exactly where did he say it would be?" Lacey persisted.

"He said it would be under the mat, but I—"

"You found it in the flowerpot, right?" She finished the sentence for him.

"Yes." It was his turn to frown. "How did you know?"

"Because that's where Margo said she would leave me the key, only I tripped over the mat and saw the key underneath it, so I didn't bother to look in the flowerpot," she explained.

There were other things she remembered, too, that backed up his claim that he had been in the house since Thursday. "It must have been your car I heard leaving on Friday morning," she murmured aloud.

"I left around six-thirty, quarter to seven," he admitted.

"And it was your orange juice glass I washed," she went on.

"I was late." She could see by the absent look in his eyes that he was recalling the events of that Friday morning, too. "I had orange juice and didn't bother with coffee until I reached my office. But I didn't see you here."

"I was out on the balcony having my morning coffee. It's all so incredible!" Lacey declared, moving blindly back to one of the sofas and sinking on to its cushions. "I went to bed early both nights and slept like a log."

"It was nearly midnight Thursday and Friday before I came in," he added.

"And when you came in tonight I thought you were a burglar." She laughed briefly.

"And I thought you were some college girl sleeping in the first empty house you found," he chuckled in return.

"What a mix-up!" Lacey shook her head. "I wonder if Bob and Margo have discovered yet that they each asked somebody to stay in the house."

"I doubt it." He walked to the fireplace, flicking the ash of his cigarette into the smoldering remains of the fire.

"I guess it doesn't matter," she sighed, smiling at the humor she could now see in the situation. "They're in Florida anyway. There isn't much they can do to put it right now. It's up to us to straighten it out."

"It's too late to do anything about it tonight." Picking up the poker, he put it back in its stand. "Tomorrow is plenty of time for you to pack."

"Me?" Lacey squeaked in astonishment.

"Naturally you." He glanced over his shoulder, seemingly surprised that Lacey didn't agree.

"Why 'naturally me?' " she demanded.

"If I'd been a burglar tonight, exactly what could you have done?" he reasoned. "There isn't a neighbor close enough to hear you scream."

"I don't care," Lacey insisted stubbornly. "I'm on vacation. This is a perfect spot and I'm not leaving."

"If it's a vacation on the beach you want, go and check into a hotel." He regarded her with infuriating calm, his roughly hewn features set in completely unrelenting lines.

"Presuming, of course, that I was able to get a reservation at this late date, I couldn't afford two weeks in a hotel," she retorted. "I'm staying here. You go."

"I'm not," he answered decisively. "Thanks to some incompetent...." He cut off that sentence abruptly and started another. "Business demands are not going to permit me the luxury of a vacation. The most I can hope for is to get away for a few hours now and then where I can't be reached by telephone. This place is ideal."

The corner of his mouth then lifted in a wry smile. "I don't even know your name."

"Andrews. Lacey Andrews."

A wicked glint of laughter sparkled in his eyes. "You are the redoubtable Miss Andrews?"

"I beg your pardon?" She tipped her head to òne side, staring at him in total confusion. Why had he put it that way?

"Where do you live?" he asked unexpectedly.

"I have a small apartment on the outskirts of Newport News. Why?" Except for that glittering light of amusement dancing in his blue eyes, his expression was impassive and enigmatic.

"Where do you work?"

*What does that have to do with anything?* Lacey thought crossly, but answered in the hope that he would eventually satisfy her curiosity.

"I'm a secretary to a construction engineer in Newport News."

The wicked glint became all the more pronounced. " 'I am not claiming Mr. Bowman is out. I am stating it,' " he mimicked unexpectedly.

# CHAPTER THREE

LACEY'S MOUTH opened and closed. "You...you aren't Mr. Whitfield, are you?" she accused with breathless incredulity.

"Cole Whitfield." He identified himself with a mocking nod of his head. "At last we meet face to face instead of via a telephone."

Stunned, Lacey stared at the tall, broad-shouldered man standing in front of the fireplace. Strong, carved features carried the stamp of a man accustomed to having authority over others. Lacey recognized that now.

His hair was brown, darker than her own, an umber shade that bordered on black. Yet there was a decided virility about him, an aura of sheer maleness that Lacey would simply never have associated with Mr. Whitfield.

Over the telephone he had been as abrasive as rough-finished steel coated with a winter morning frost. Her mind's image of Mr. Whitfield did not resemble this vital, compelling man at all. Lacey was still gaping when his firmly molded mouth moved to speak.

"Don't I come up to your expectations?" he asked mockingly.

She found her voice long enough to croak, "Hardly."

"What did you think I would be? An ogre with three heads?" Cole Whitfield inquired, his voice husky with contained amusement. "I left the other two heads at the office."

"You are the rudest, most caustic man...." Lacey began, quite evenly, to describe the man she had known as Cole Whitfield.

"If you had as much money, mine and investors', tied up in that building as I do and had suffered the delays that I have, you'd be snapping at everyone, too," he interrupted without a trace of apology for his behavior.

"And that's your excuse?" she declared indignantly.

"No, it doesn't excuse my attitude, Lacey." Cole Whitfield used her Christian name with ease. "But it does explain why I'm in such desperate need for some peace and quiet before it becomes impossible for me to live with myself. By the way—" his deeply blue eyes were laughing again "—did you ever find those toilets?"

"I know quite a few places where they're not, but there's a tracer out on the shipment." A smile tugged at the corners of her mouth, but she refused to let it show. She hadn't completely forgiven him for his rudeness. "There should be a more definite word by Monday afternoon."

"But you're on vacation, so you won't be there." He tossed his cigarette into the fireplace, momentarily releasing Lacey from his vaguely disturbing gaze. "Which brings us back to our present impasse."

"Who stays and who goes." Her chin jutted forward to an angle of battle.

Cole Whitfield saw it and rested an elbow on the mantelpiece, an indolent gesture that seemed to indicate his own entrenchment.

"Since we're both prepared to be stubborn, I think the solution is for both of us to stay." Lacey arched an eyebrow, more in surprise than rejection of his proposal. "After all, we've already spent two nights together under the same roof," he reminded her.

There was one point she wanted clarified before she considered his suggestion seriously. "Are you rephrasing your invitation to share your empty bed?" she questioned frankly.

"You are alluding to my comment earlier, aren't you?" He smiled. "At the time, you struck me as being a slightly naive and frightened college girl, and propositioning you seemed the quickest way of making you take flight." There was a brief, negative shake of his head. "I'm not interested in sex. I'm here for the peace and quiet. Although—" his gaze skimmed over her scantily clad figure "—if you make a habit of wandering around in that state of near-undress, I might exercise a woman's prerogative and change my mind," he added with a mocking inflection in his voice.

His allusion to her sex sent an odd tremor quaking through her nerve ends. Hastily she raised the drooping neckline of her pajama top and tucked the torn strap under her arm, but there was nothing she could do about the brevity of her nightclothes or the bare expanse of shapely leg and thigh they revealed.

"Part of it's your fault," she retorted defensively, referring to the torn strap.

"Entirely by accident," he assured her. "Well, what do you say?"

"You just said you wanted peace and quiet. Why are you willing to have me stay here, too?" Lacey wanted to know.

"My previous encounters with you may have been brief, but they left me with a lasting impression. If I tried to insist that you leave, I'm certain you would fight to the last breath, and I've had all the fighting and arguing that I want. Besides, I'm tired," he admitted, and Lacey noticed the lines of strain around his mouth. "I would much rather come to an amicable arrangement that would suit both of us. We're civilized adults. You are an adult, aren't you?" he asked sarcastically.

"I'm twenty-four," she declared.

Again he gave her the once-over. "You look older."

"Thanks a lot!" A faintly angered astonishment ran through her voice. She was usually accused of not looking her age instead of the other way around.

"Probably wishful thinking on my part," he sighed tiredly, and looked away. "It's just that you look so damned seductive sitting there like that."

An uncomfortable flush warmed her cheeks. "I'll get a robe," she murmured, and started to scramble off the sofa, tightly clutching the bodice of her pajamas.

Cole Whitfield moved to block her path. "Don't bother."

Immediately his mouth thinned impatiently. "What I mean is—" he started to put his hands on her shoulders, then stiffly drew them back to his side "—if you agree with my solution, there's no reason why we can't turn in for the night. In separate rooms, of course," he joked tightly.

"I. . . ." Lacey hesitated.

At close quarters, his inherent virility suddenly held a powerful attraction. And if, as he had implied, he had felt a similar reaction to her, wouldn't rooming together

under a supposedly platonic agreement prove to be volatile and unworkable?

"I know what you're thinking," he said quietly—and
strangely Lacey believed that he did. "Things could
only get sticky if we let them. I may be ill-tempered at
times, but I still have control over my baser instincts.
And so, I'm sure, do you."

He was right. A smile flickered over her lips as she
found humor in her silly apprehensions. They were both
adults. The situation couldn't get out of hand unless
they permitted it.

"Does that smile mean yes, roommate?" The corners
of his eyes crinkled, although the line of his mouth remained straight.

"Yes," she nodded.

"Fine. Then what do you say we bring this conversation to an end so I can get some sleep?" Cole Whitfield
suggested lazily.

"Right." Lacey smiled. "Good night," she said, and
moved past him to the hallway leading to her bedroom.

Three-quarters of an hour later she was lying in
her bed, dead tired yet unable to fall asleep. She
fought to lie still and not toss and turn with her restless-
ness.

The previous two nights, when she hadn't known
Cole Whitfield was sleeping in the next room, she had
slept like a baby. But now, knowing he was there, she
discovered she wasn't quite as nonchalant about it as
she had thought she would be. Good grief, she could
even hear the squeak of his bedsprings when he moved.

*You're being immature,* she scolded herself silently,
and forced her eyes to close.

IT WAS A LONG TIME before she was able to ignore his presence in the house and drift into sleep. In consequence it was past midmorning before she awakened, vaguely irritable from having slept too late.

Grabbing her cotton housecoat from the foot of the bed, she pulled it on as she hurried toward the bathroom. In the hall she stopped face to face with a bleary-eyed, tousle-haired Cole, also en route to the bathroom.

His dark blue eyes made a disgruntled sweep of her and she felt a moment's relief that she had changed into her long-legged silky pajamas of turquoise blue. He couldn't accuse her of not being substantially covered!

The same couldn't be said for him, she realized as she became rather painfully conscious that below that naked expanse of his tanned chest he was wearing a pair of jockey shorts. She had often seen her two older brothers similarly attired, yet it wasn't quite the same when the man was Cole Whitfield.

There was a sardonic twist of his mouth as he gestured toward the bathroom door. "Ladies first." Then he retreated unself-consciously into the second guest room.

Lacey darted into the bathroom, her cheeks burning like a schoolgirl's. Cold water from the tap was more effective than the silent chiding words she directed at herself. With her face washed, teeth brushed, and light makeup applied, she emerged from the bathroom.

A glance into Cole's room saw him sitting on the edge of the unmade bed, his dark head resting tiredly in his hands.

"I'm all through," Lacey told him, with considerably more poise regarding his state of dress. "It's yours now. I'm going to put some coffee on to perk."

"Good." He sighed deeply, rubbing his hands over his face before rising.

In the kitchen, she filled the coffee pot with water and spooned fresh grounds into the basket. Water was running in the shower when she plugged the electric percolator in. She had plenty of time to dress before Cole was finished in the bathroom, so she poured a glass of orange juice and climbed on to one of the tall stools at the counter to drink it.

As she finished the juice, she heard the water being turned off in the shower. Sighing, she slid from the stool and started to her room.

She was halfway across the living room when the front doorbell rang. Changing her direction to answer it, she shrugged. It was probably someone to see Margo and Bob.

Descending the steps, she paused at the front door to look out through the peephole. A man and a woman stood outside, but Lacey couldn't see enough of them to recognize them as anyone she knew. She opened the door a crack.

"Yes?" She smiled politely at the pair.

They were complete strangers to her. The woman had beautiful long wheat blond hair, and makeup precisely applied to her striking features. Her green eyes registered shock at the sight of Lacey standing on the other side of the door.

Her clothes were casual, white slacks with a vividly red print top. On the blonde they looked chic—the only adjective Lacey could find to describe her impression.

The man, taller with sandy blond hair, seemed first surprised to see Lacey, then amused. He was very good-looking, but she suspected he was probably conceitedly aware of the fact.

She opened her mouth to explain that Bob and Margo were on vacation, but the woman spoke before she had the chance.

"We must have the wrong address, Vic," she declared in an icy tone. She would have turned to leave if the man hadn't taken hold of her elbow to keep her at the door.

Without glancing at the blonde, he directed his curious gaze at Lacey. "We're looking for Cole Whitfield. Is he here?"

Lacey became tense, suddenly aware of all the embarrassing connotations that could be read into her presence in the house alone with Cole all night. But what did it matter? She had done nothing to be ashamed of, so why act like it?

"He's here." She opened the door wide to let the couple in. "Follow me."

She started up the stairs with the unnaturally silent pair behind her. Just for a minute Lacey wished she had dressed instead of having orange juice, but it was too late now.

As they passed the landing, the attractive blonde asked with a somewhat superior air, "Are you the housekeeper?"

To any other question Lacey would have probably answered politely, with an explanation of the circumstances for her being in the house. But that one grated. She half turned on the stairs, a hand on her hip, and gave the woman a deliberately cool and amused look.

"Do I look like a housekeeper to you?"

Without waiting for a reply she started up the stairs
again. She could feel the blonde's freezing anger as surely as if a cold north wind were blowing.

Behind her she heard the man murmur very quietly
and with considerable mockery, "You were really
reaching for straws with that question, Monica."

"Shut up!" was the hissing reply.

In the living room Lacey paused near the sofa. She
was about to suggest that the pair take a seat while she
went to tell Cole they were here. At that same instant,
she heard the bathroom door open.

"Lacey!" There was a savage bite in the way Cole
called her name. Her head jerked at the sound, hearing
his strides carrying him toward the living room.

"Have you been using my razor?" he demanded angrily, rounding the hall to stop short at the sight of the
three people staring at him.

A white terry cloth towel was wrapped around his
waist. A smaller hand towel was draped around his
neck. His hair was glistening darkly from the shower
and shaving lather covered his tanned face, except for
one small strip that had been shaved away, revealing a
telltale dot of red to indicate he had nicked himself with
the blade.

Despite his abrupt halt upon entering the living room,
he made no other outward sign that the appearance of
his visitors had upset him in any way. His blue gaze was
only faintly narrowed as it flicked from the woman to
the man to Lacey.

Lifting a corner of the towel around his neck, he
pressed it to the nick near his jaw. He seemed to expect a
response from Lacey to his initial question.

"If you used the razor that was lying on the shelf above the sink, it was mine," she answered smoothly. "Yours is in the cabinet."

Her reply appeared to snap the thin thread of control the blonde had on her temper. "Cole, I want to know who this woman is and what she's doing here!" Her voice trembled violently.

"And good morning to you, too, Monica. Yes, it is a lovely day." The smile curving Cole's mouth was faintly sarcastic. He removed the towel from around his neck and began wiping away the foamy lather drying on his face.

"I think you'd better excuse me," Lacey inserted, certain she was witnessing only the first eruption from the attractive and obviously volatile blonde.

"Is the coffee done?" Cole asked. "I could use a cup."

"I think so," Lacey admitted.

He had partially cut off her retreat with his request. She had thought he would want an opportunity to explain in private the reason she was there, but evidently he didn't.

"Hello, Vic. How have you been?" Cole directed his calmly conversational remark to the man with the blonde as Lacey walked to the kitchen.

"Not bad, Cole. Not bad," was the reply.

But Lacey could hear the underlying laughter in the man's voice. She had no idea what the relationship was between the blonde and her escort, but it was fairly plain that he found a great deal of humor in the situation.

As she started to pour the coffee, a sobering thought

occurred to her. Whoever the woman was, she believed she had a right to an explanation from Cole. And Lacey realized that she had no idea whether Cole was married or not.

Good lord! What if the woman was his wife? She nearly dropped the coffee pot, the color rushing from her face.

"You haven't answered my question, Cole," the blonde whom Cole had addressed as Monica reminded him in an icily enraged tone.

"I didn't think you really expected an answer," he replied in a deadly low voice. "I was certain you had it all worked out for yourself."

The cup clattered rather noisily in its saucer as Lacey carried it into the living room to Cole. Her complexion was unnaturally pale, her color not completely regained from the shocking possibility that had occurred to her.

The three were still standing, Cole and Monica eyeing each other with almost open hostility. Lacey came up to Cole's side, offering him the coffee she had poured. The cup ceased its rattling the instant he took it from her hand to set it on the nearest table.

"Aren't you going to introduce us, Cole?" the sandy-haired Vic prodded, gazing intently at Lacey.

A muscular arm curved lightly and possessively around the back of her waist, and she stiffened in resistance to Cole's touch. Her gaze flashed to his, meeting the bland glitter of his unusually dark blue eyes.

She heard the other woman's savagely indrawn breath, which resembled a cat's hiss, her green eyes glowing with hatred. And she realized that Cole was deliberately goading the woman, further incensing her with his action rather than trying to smooth her ruffled fur.

"You haven't formally met my roommate, have you?" His steel blue gaze swung to the couple, his arm tightening around Lacey's waist when she would have drawn away.

He had referred to her as his roommate last night in a joking sense, but his use of it now was provoking and suggestive. He propelled her stiffly resisting figure a few steps forward.

"Lacey, I would like you to meet Monica Hamilton and her brother Vic Hamilton." He identified them only by name without any explanation as to his relationship to either of them. "This is Lacey Andrews."

Monica merely gave Lacey a green look of hatred, but her brother reached to shake her hand. "It's definitely a pleasure to meet you, Lacey," he murmured.

He retained his hold of her hand. The look he gave her made Lacey feel as if she were wearing a black negligee instead of being so fully covered by long pajamas and her housecoat.

"Back off, Vic," Cole ordered quietly.

Lacey's hand was released as Vic smiled mockingly from her to Cole. "I see, private property—no trespassing, is that it?"

"That's it," Cole agreed with a curt nod.

"Don't you think," Lacey suggested stiffly, "that you should explain to your friends the exact circumstances for my being here, Cole?" As far as she was concerned this farce had continued much too long already.

He glanced at her, seeing her rigid with anger. "

don't think Monica is interested in learning how you came to be here, Lacey," he replied drolly. "Nor a description of what happened between us last night. She's seen all the evidence with her own eyes and filled in all the sordid details with her imagination."

"Tell her," Lacey insisted.

With a mild shrug of acquiescence, he swung his gaze to Monica. "Despite the way it looks, this is all perfectly innocent," he told her. "As a matter of fact, Lacey and I slept in separate beds."

"Before or after?" Monica snapped.

There was an I-told-you-so glint in his eyes when he glanced back at Lacey, and she acknowledged silently that Monica was beyond listening to any explanation at this time. And Cole was to blame for that.

There was a challenge in the set of his jaw when he again reverted his attention to Monica. "You haven't mentioned why you're here."

"We came to invite you to dinner and arrange an impromptu beach party for this afternoon," she replied caustically. "Of course, I was under the impression that you were here alone with nothing to do all day."

"Obviously you were wrong," Cole returned with a complacent smile.

His arm tightened unexpectedly around Lacey's waist, drawing her more fully against his side before she could make a move to stop him.

"Don't!" she protested in a low angry whisper.

By the time his grip lessened, it was too late. Monica was already turning on her heel, her long blond hair swinging around her shoulders.

"We're going, Vic," she snapped.

"I'll see you, Cole," Vic shrugged, but it was Lacey he was looking at before he turned to follow his sister.

"Monica, do you remember what I told you the other day?" Cole's voice halted her at the top of the stairs, her attractive features haughty with pride. "I think you understand now that I meant it when I said, 'Don't call me, I'll call you.' "

Liquid green eyes shimmered briefly and resentfully at Lacey. Then Monica was descending the stairs with a faintly smiling Vic behind her. Neither Lacey nor Cole moved or spoke until they heard the front door shut.

"You shou—" Lacey began reprovingly.

But the deep, rich laughter coming from his throat stunned her into silence. The hand resting lightly on the back of her waist suddenly exerted pressure to sweep her against his chest.

"You're a godsend, Lacey!" he laughed.

In the next second, his mouth was swooping down to claim her lips in a hard, sure kiss that took her breath away. When he lifted his head to study her, her reaction was chaotic.

The firm imprint of his mouth still tingled on her lips, the scent of soap and shaving cream assailing her nose. Her heart was tripping over itself, unable to find its normal beat. Over all that, confusion reigned at his lightning change from sarcastic coldness with Monica to this warm, hearty amusement.

He locked his hands together at the small of her back. Lacey's own fingers were spread across his chest in mute protest, aware of the solidness of his naked flesh.

His wickedly glinting eyes looked deeply into hers,

crinkling at the corners while taking note of the confusion darkening her brown eyes.

"I've been trying to get that attractive crow off my back for several months," he explained. "I think the sight of you scared her off for good. For that, you possess my undying gratitude."

"Who is she?" Lacey frowned.

"A couple of years ago I briefly, and unwisely, made her my fiancée. I soon rectified that mistake, but Monica isn't the type to take rejection lightly. In fact, she's been trying to persuade me to change my mind ever since I broke our engagement." His face was disconcertingly near hers, the chiseled male contours shadowed by the overnight beard growth.

"So that's why you deliberately let her believe we'd spent the night together—in the intimate sense," Lacey said, half in accusation and half in conclusion.

"Exactly. She wouldn't have believed me if I'd tried to convince her otherwise," Cole insisted calmly. "Knowing the way her mind works, if there'd been a motion picture camera hidden in the house to film all that happened—or failed to happen—last night, she still would have been certain that I'd somehow messed up the film."

Lacey wriggled free of his unrestraining hold, finding his nearness just a little too disturbing, especially when he was only half-clothed. She moved a few feet away under his watchful yet mellow gaze.

"I am sorry, though," he added. "It wasn't really fair to involve you, not when you're an innocent bystander." A smile tugged at the edge of his mouth, deepening the cleft in his chin. "I hope you don't mind being unjustly branded as a scarlet woman."

"Spending a night with a man in today's society doesn't put a scarlet stain on a girl anymore," Lacey answered, adultly shrugging away the suggestion. "To be honest, I thought for a moment that she was your wife, and I was more worried about being named a correspondent in some divorce suit."

Cole winced mockingly. "Please don't remind me how close I came to having Monica for my wife. A man doesn't like to believe he was ever that much of a fool."

"She's very beautiful," Lacey commented absently, picturing the green eyed blonde in her mind.

"If ever the saying 'Beauty is as beauty does' is true, it is when it's applied to Monica," Cole stated. Then he asked unexpectedly, "Can you cook?"

It took Lacey a second to follow his rapid change of the subject. "I'm about average—definitely not cordon bleu. Why?"

"I'm hungry and I was hoping I could persuade you to fix breakfast," he grinned.

"I think first I'll get dressed," she replied, adding silently to herself, *before any more visitors show up*.

Cole rubbed the stubble on his chin. "And I still have to shave. You said my razor was in the cabinet?"

Lacey nodded. "I noticed it there this morning."

She was only a step behind him as he started down the hallway. When he stopped at the bathroom door, she started to walk by him to her bedroom, but he laid a hand on her forearm to stop her.

"I want you to know that I didn't mean this to happen this morning," he told her, a serious frown drawing his dark brows together. "When I made the suggestion last night that we both stay here, I had no plan whatsoever to use you to get rid of Monica."

"I believe that," she assured him. "It never occurred to me that you might have."

"I hope not." Cole paused for a second. "If I'd known she was coming over this morning, I would have insisted you leave rather than have you the subject of her vile suspicions."

"It doesn't matter." Lacey didn't want to dwell on Monica's suspicions. "Would you like bacon or sausage with your eggs?" she asked, using his tactic of changing the subject.

"Bacon—crisp," he smiled, aware of what she was doing. "And three poached eggs on a slice of dark toast."

"I was asking your preference, not taking your order," she sighed with mocking exasperation.

His smile deepened for a teasing minute before he walked into the bathroom and closed the door. Lacey stared at the white woodwork, then moved to her own bedroom.

Cole Whitfield. The man in person was vastly different from the ill-tempered voice on the telephone. This Cole Whitfield she could like.

# CHAPTER FOUR

THE BACON WAS already fried and draining on a paper towel when Cole wandered into the kitchen-dining area. Lacey lifted the poached eggs onto the dark toast.

"Looks good." He reached across the counter bar to take the plate from her hand.

Lacey hoped the food tasted good, but she didn't say so. "The silverware, salt and pepper are already on the table. Coffee to drink or would you like something else?"

"Coffee is fine." He moved to the table where a place setting and a clean cup were laid. Lacey brought him the plate of bacon, as well as the coffee pot to fill his cup. He glanced around the table, then at her. "Aren't you eating?"

"Just a slice of toast." She walked back to the kitchen area for her coffee cup and the small plate with additional slices of toast on it, one for her and the rest for him.

"Are you watching your figure?" There was something mocking in the sweeping look he gave her as she turned to rejoin him. Lacey hoped it implied that there was nothing wrong with her shape.

"No," she said. "I thought I'd go for a swim, so I didn't want anything heavy in my stomach."

She had expected him to say he would come with her, but he only nodded at her statement. Lacey wondered what he planned to do but decided it was better not to pry. After all, nobody liked a nosy roommate.

The colored bamboo blinds at the dining-room windows were raised, letting in the morning sunlight. Lacey nibbled at her toast and gazed at the ocean view of sparkling waves and brilliant gold beaches.

"How long have you worked for Bowman?" Cole asked with apparent casualness.

"I've worked for the firm for almost five years and for M...Mr. Bowman the past two." Despite her unusual living arrangement with Cole, Lacey decided it was wiser if he wasn't aware Mike was a friend as well as her boss.

"You must have gone to work for the company straight out of school," he commented.

"Straight out of secretarial school," she said, qualifying his answer.

"Did you attend school here?"

"No, in Richmond. That's where I lived— vhere my family still lives." Lacey dunked the last bite of toast in her coffee.

"What made you decide to come here to work? There must have been plenty of openings in Richmond where you could be with your family and friends." He eyed her curiously.

"That age-old desire to leave home and be totally on my own." She shrugged and cupped a hand under the dripping piece of toast to carry it to her mouth.

It occurred to her that she had the perfect opening to ask him about his family and background. But by the time she was able to swallow the food in her mouth, it was too late to take advantage of it.

"You're a very good cook," Cole stated. "Remind me to recommend you if you ever decide to change your profession to chef."

"Thank you." Lacey was ridiculously pleased by his compliment and tried not to show it.

He pushed his plate to the side and leaned back in his chair. "Since you did the cooking, I guess it's only fair that I wash the dishes."

"I...." She was about to insist that she would clean up, then decided she would fast turn into his maid if she wasn't careful. And that wasn't the way she intended to spend her vacation. "All right," she agreed.

"What? No protest?" Laughter danced in his deep blue eyes.

"No protest. I hate washing dishes." Lacey rose from the table before she succumbed to the old-fashioned notion that doing dishes wasn't man's work. "I'm going for my swim. Have fun."

In her room, Lacey stripped off her slacks and knit top down to the bathing suit beneath. The suit was the promised vacation present to herself. Its slick material gave its blue gray color a metallic sheen and molded itself to her slender figure like a second skin.

Draping a beach towel around her shoulders, she closed the door to her room behind her. Lacey avoided the kitchen, where she could hear water running in the sink, and slipped out through the glass-paneled balcony doors to the steps leading down to the beach.

The water was cool. Lacey had second thoughts about her swim, her skin shivering as she immersed herself in the waves. But after some vigorous strokes, striking a parallel line to the beach, she soon became acclimatized to the temperature of the water and relaxed to do a bit of body-surfing.

Floating buoyantly, Lacey let the wave carry her toward shore. Before she scraped bottom, she righted herself and started to wade back to deeper water. As she made her turn seaward, she saw Cole farther down the beach. In hip boots, he was casting a fishing line into the surf. At least she had her answer as to what he planned to do and why he hadn't mentioned joining her for a swim.

An hour later, she decided she'd had enough of the sun and sea for a while and waded onto the beach. Shaking the sand out of her towel, she dried herself off and glanced toward Cole. He lifted a hand in greeting and she waved back.

"Having any luck?" she called.

He shook his head and shouted back, "None!"

It wasn't a response that encouraged more conversation and Lacey walked back alone to the beach house. A shower washed away the ocean salt and shampoo cleaned her hair. Dressed in fresh clothes, Lacey rinsed out her swimsuit and hung it over a towel rack in the bathroom to dry.

She wandered onto the balcony, leaning a hip against the rail while she idly toweled her short hair damp-dry. After several minutes, she hung the towel over the rail. The afternoon sun could finish drying her hair, she decided, and haphazardly combed the strands into order with her fingers.

She could see, up the beach some distance away, Cole

still engrossed in his fishing, apparently in the same spot as before. She thought back to their extremely brief exchange when she ended her swim.

Of course, Lacey hadn't expected him to suddenly turn into her companion just because they were temporarily staying in the same house. It was just—she sighed inwardly—it would have been nice to sit and chat with him for a while.

But she also remembered his statement that he was there for the peace and quiet. That was why she hadn't forced her company upon him. It had just seemed right and proper that she should respect his wishes.

As she watched him, Lacey saw him pick up his pole and tackle box and start down the long stretch of beach toward the house. She darted into the house to the bathroom, where she quickly ran a comb through her nearly dry hair and added a touch of strawberry gloss to her lips.

Inwardly she was laughing at herself all the while she was doing it, because it was quite laughable to think she might want to impress Cole. She was just stepping onto the balcony again when the doorbell rang.

Her first thought was that it was Monica returning for some nefarious reason, and she glanced toward the beach to see Cole still a considerable distance away. Then, shrugging in resignation that she would have to face the green-eyed lioness alone, she walked unhurriedly into the house and down the stairs to answer the door.

But it was Mike Bowman who was standing outside when she opened the door, and her brown eyes widened in surprise at the sight of him. He gave her a crooked smile.

"It took you long enough to answer the door," he teased good-naturedly. "I was beginning to think either I had the wrong house or you'd gone somewhere."

"Hello, Mike," Lacey murmured, not fully recovered from the shock.

He waited patiently for her to invite him in. When she continued to stare at him, he tilted his head to one side in an inquiring fashion.

"You did invite me over this afternoon, or have you forgotten?" he prompted gently.

An embarrassed pink rouged her cheeks. "I didn't forget," she lied rather than admit it had completely slipped her mind that she had asked him over this afternoon. "I simply wasn't expecting you so soon." Glancing down at her beige checked shorts and the orange midriff top, she tried to pretend it was a concern for her dress that had caused her to look so uncomfortable. "I'm not dressed or anything." She lifted a hand to her shining crown of silky brown hair. "And my hair isn't even all the way dry."

"You look great to me," Mike insisted. "Are you going to invite me in or do you want me to wait in the car until you're ready?" he teased as she continued to block the doorway.

"Do you see how flustered you've made me?" Lacey forced a laugh. She swung the door wider and stepped away to let him in.

Actually, she knew exactly why she was so flustered. In a minute she would have to explain to him about Cole Whitfield's living in the same house with her.

The situation was bizarre enough to her. She wasn't certain how Mike would react to it or exactly how she would go about telling him, considering the biting things she had said about Cole in Mike's company.

As she led the way up the steps, she was still trying to decide whether she should just blurt it out or make a joke out of it or what. One thing was certain—she had to make up her mind pretty soon or Cole would be walking in and the whole thing would be out in the open before she could prepare Mike for the news. The entire situation was becoming more complicated by the minute.

"This is quite a place," Mike declared as they reached the top of the stairs and entered the living room.

"It is beautiful," Lacey agreed absently, and began, "Mike, I—"

"It's custom-built, isn't it?" He surveyed the room, his gaze narrowing as he studied its construction.

"I believe so. I—"

"It shows," he nodded. "I don't see anything that looks at all slipshod. And that fireplace is a masterpiece." He smiled at her. "No wonder you so readily accepted your cousin's request to stay here while she was gone. Oh—" he suddenly remembered the sack he carried "—here're the steaks I promised to bring. I had the butcher cut them special. He promised they'd be so tender you could cut them with a fork. There's also a bottle of wine in here." He handed the sack to Lacey. "You'll probably want to open it so it can warm a bit before we eat."

"Yes, I will." She started toward the kitchen, certain that Mike was following her. "Mike, there's something I have to tell you."

Setting the sack on the counter, she waited for him to

ask what. But when she glanced around, he wasn't anywhere in sight.

"Mike?" She took the bottle of wine from the sack and opened it. Looking around again, she saw the door to the balcony standing open and hurried to it.

"This is some view," he commented, turning as he heard her approach.

"It is spectacular." Lacey rushed on before he could interrupt, "There's something I have to explain to you."

"Look!" He pointed out to sea. "See that ship way out there?"

Lacey glimpsed the silhouette of a large ocean-going vessel on the horizon. She saw it strictly by accident as she scanned the beach and the path to the house for Cole. He was nowhere in sight. She felt as if she were sitting on a time bomb with the seconds ticking away.

"This is impressive," Mike nodded, his gaze sliding to the beach. "You practically have this whole area to yourself."

"Not exactly," Lacey qualified. "I—"

"It's fairly isolated," he reminded her. "Does it bother you to be here alone?"

This was her opening. "Not a bit, because I'm not—"

"Lacey!" Cole's voice sliced off the end of her sentence. She froze as Mike jerked his gaze to the interior of the house. "I rummaged around the garage and found Bob's grill." His voice was coming steadily nearer to the balcony door. "I decided that since you fixed breakfast this morning, it's only fair that I cook dinner."

The time bomb had exploded. Lacey saw the shock

waves reverberating through Mike as Cole stepped onto the balcony carrying the charcoal grill.

Cole stopped, drawing his head back when he saw Mike. "Bowman," he identified him before his questioning blue eyes swung to Lacey.

"I invited him over for dinner." She didn't add that she had forgotten. It was written in the look she gave Cole.

Cole set the grill down. "I know the way this must look to you, Bowman, but, believe me, it's really quite innocent."

"Are you staying here, Whitfield?" Mike frowned, his voice lifting to a pitch of disbelief.

"I was going to tell you," Lacey inserted, trying desperately not to sound guilty.

"I see." He sounded grimly skeptical.

"I don't think you do," Cole joined in. "You see, there was a mix-up. Lacey's cousin asked her to stay in the house and her husband asked me. When Lacey and I discovered what had happened—" he fortunately didn't explain the circumstances of their discovery "—we couldn't decide which of us would leave. Finally we mutually agreed that we would both stay."

"Do you mean—" Mike's frown deepened "—you two are living in this house together?"

"I was trying to find a way to tell you," Lacey repeated, sensing his rising anger, "so that it wouldn't sound as if we'd come to some illicit arrangement."

"We're sharing the house, not the beds," Cole stated bluntly.

Mike turned away, rubbing the back of his neck. "I don't believe this," he muttered beneath his breath.

He glanced bewilderedly at Lacey. "You're actually living with the same man that just last week I heard you wish would take a flying leap into a dry lake?"

Her darting look at Cole saw his mouth twitch with amusement, a mocking glitter in his blue eyes. Even though she hadn't made any secret of her previous opinion of Cole, she wished Mike hadn't repeated her words.

"I think it will be better if the two of you talk this thing out on your own, so I'll make myself scarce." Cole nodded briefly to Lacey, a rueful smile of apology touching the firm line of his mouth.

Lacey nodded her agreement to his suggestion, but offered no words of goodbye. She couldn't very well say "I'll see you later"—not without aggravating the situation.

His departure left an uneasy silence in his wake. Below her, Lacey could hear the opening of the garage door, followed by the sound of Cole's car reversing into the driveway. She glanced at Mike's profile, determined not to apologize for this situation that was so completely innocent.

"I can't believe you've actually agreed to this," Mike declared, slapping his palm on the railing in a mixture of anger and confusion.

"Honestly, Mike," Lacey sighed, "you make it sound as though I've suddenly deserted to the enemy camp! It isn't like that at all."

"I know," he admitted grudgingly. "It was just such a shock, seeing Whitfield here with you, then finding out that the two of you are living together."

Lacey bridled at his continued use of that term to

describe their arrangement. "You wouldn't consider it living together if we were both living in the same apartment building or staying in the same hotel. This isn't any different."

"It doesn't matter how you put it, Lacey," Mike retorted, "sharing a house is not the same as living in the same building. Good God, you cooked breakfast for the man. You don't do that for someone who is only living under the same roof."

"That's not the way I see it."

"You're a fool," he muttered beneath his breath.

"Look, we can argue about this all night, but I'm not going to change my mind," Lacey flashed, her chin stubbornly thrust forward.

Mike turned from the rail to confront her. "What do you want me to do, Lacey? Do you want me to leave?" he challenged. "It's apparent that you forgot you invited me today, so if you'd rather forget about dinner, I'll go."

"I don't want to forget about dinner," she insisted, because she didn't want to give Mike the impression that she preferred Cole's company for the evening—a conclusion he would surely reach no matter how she tried to deny it. "I want you to stay for dinner—as long as you agree to drop this subject. After all, you don't have any right to criticize my behavior."

Breathing in deeply, he eyed her for several seconds. "All right," he agreed tautly. "No more discussion about this."

Pretending that something didn't exist didn't make it go away. It was like sweeping dirt under the rug: it couldn't be seen, but it was still there. Subsequently it

was one of the most miserable afternoons and evenings
Lacey had ever spent. The atmosphere had crackled
with Mike's disapproval, stringing Lacey's nerves to a
fine tension.

They were both relieved when he left early. The time
they had spent together had been uncomfortable rather
than like the companionable good times they had previously known. Even after he had left, Lacey remained
irritated with Mike for making her feel guilty about a
situation that was completely innocent.

She walked the beach to try to rid herself of her inner
agitation with no success. The rush of the surf did not
soothe her nerves. There was no magic in the play of the
moonlight on the ocean swells. The tangy salt breeze
didn't change the sour taste in her mouth. Finally Lacey
returned to the house, but the vision of the night's dinner haunted her. She chose to stare out the window at
the empty beach.

Absently she heard the sound of a car driving into the
garage, but it was Cole's footsteps on the stairs that
finally broke her brooding stance in front of the windows facing the ocean.

She remembered too late that she had intended to be
in bed before Cole returned. She glanced at the watch
on her wrist. It was nearly eleven. She turned as Cole
paused at the top of the stairs to glance around.

"Bowman's left?" he asked for her confirmation.

"A couple, three hours ago," acknowledged Lacey,
unaware of the vaguely dejected note that had crept into
her voice.

His gaze became fixed on her, the electric blue of his
eyes so intent that she had to turn away, afraid of what

he might be seeing. There was an uneasy feeling in the pit of her stomach. A nervous reaction to the night's tension, she told herself.

"It didn't go very well with Bowman, did it?" Cole observed, crossing the room to where Lacey stood.

She blinked at him in surprise, then had to look away again to avoid the disturbing study of his eyes. He was much too observant and astute. As he stood tall beside her, tanned and vital, she also had to admit that he was rather overpoweringly male.

"No, it didn't," she answered truthfully.

"Didn't he believe you?"

"Mike believed that the arrangement was all perfectly innocent all right." Lacey laughed shortly without humor. "He just doesn't approve."

"I suppose you argued and that's why he left so early?"

Lacey shook her head in denial. "We didn't argue."

Maybe it would have been better if they had, but it would have meant an open breach between them. After tonight, she guessed that they would just drift apart—be employer and employee and nothing more. In a way it was sad that it was going to turn out that way.

"I knew you worked for Bowman, but it never occurred to me that you were going with him," Cole mused.

Her sideways glance observed him gazing out to sea, a thoughtful expression on his bluntly carved features. The suggestion of grimness around his mouth made her want to reach out with her fingers and smooth it away. It reminded her too much of the autocratic Mr. Whitfield who had so often infuriated her over the telephone.

"It's nothing serious between Mike and me," she said, correcting his impression that she was going with Mike. "We've dated a few times, that's all. It isn't likely to develop into any more than that, either."

"Because of tonight?" Again the dark blue eyes were studying her profile, alert to any nuance in her expression.

"No, not really." Which was true. "Mike just naturally shies away from any relationship that starts to become serious. I think you can truly say he's a confirmed bachelor." Lacey smiled.

"And that doesn't bother you?" An eyebrow flicked upward in curiosity.

"No. I enjoy working with Mike and he's good company away from the office—no more than that." A breeze stirred the edge of the drawn curtain, briefly ruffling the hair curling near her ear.

Out of the corner of her eye, Lacey saw Cole stifling a yawn with the back of his hand. She felt a twinge of guilt. He had stayed away to give her and Mike some time alone. He had probably intended to have an early night after a quiet, relaxing day.

"You'd better get some sleep," she suggested. "You have to work tomorrow."

"Are you calling it a night?" he questioned, tiredly rubbing his neck.

"Mmm, I don't think so." A smile flitted across her lips. She wasn't sleepy. "I'm not the least bit tired, and since I'm on my vacation, I can sleep as late as I want in the morning. I think I'll go out on the balcony for a while and enjoy the night air."

Cole didn't move as she stepped past him to the glass-paned balcony door. She strolled to the railing, leaning both hands on it as she gazed at the moon-silvered rippling of the ocean's waves.

It was a warm, languid night spiced with the tang of salt air. A firm tread sounded on the board planks of the balcony and she glanced over her shoulder, momentarily surprised to see Cole join her at the railing. She had thought he was turning in for the night.

"What's the matter, Lacey?" he asked quietly.

"What's the matter?" she repeated blankly, and faked a laugh. "Nothing is wrong."

"Isn't it?" persisted Cole.

His dark eyes were as midnight blue as the sky, shimmering with mysterious, indistinguishable flecks of starlight. They seemed fathomless to Lacey, and disconcerting as they remained steadfastly focused on her face.

"I don't know what you mean." She stared straight ahead, fixing her attention on the gleaming path of moonlight on the water.

"Don't you?" His fingers caught her chin and turned her head toward his searching gaze.

"When I walked in tonight, I could tell something was bothering you. At first I thought it was because you and Bowman had argued, but you corrected that impression. So it must be something else that's troubling you, and I'd like to know what it is."

"It has nothing to do with you." Lacey tried to twist away from his fingers, but Cole increased the pressure to keep her facing him.

"I think it has something to do with me," he argued quietly. "Indirectly perhaps, but I'm guessing that it's about our arrangement. Am I right?"

Lacey sighed in defeat. She swore he could partially read her mind, and she didn't know whether she liked that or not.

"It's silly," she protested.

"Why don't you tell me about it?" Cole let his hand slide from her chin to rest casually on her shoulder.

"It's just that I'm slowly beginning to realize I'm not quite as liberal and freethinking as I thought I was," Lacey conceded. "I never thought other people's opinions would bother me as long as I believed that what I was doing was right. I'm finding out that I'm a bit more old-fashioned and traditional than I thought."

"Because of Monica's and Vic's reaction to our sharing the house. And Bowman's disapproval, as well," Cole concluded.

"More or less," she nodded, her dark brown hair catching and reflecting the sheen of the moonlight. "I mean, I know it's perfectly innocent," she insisted forcefully.

"So now you're having second thoughts about staying here," Cole finished.

"Oh, no, I'm not." Lacey laughed, a tremulous sound. "I bet you were hoping that's what I would say, then you could have that big fat moon all to yourself." She flicked a glance toward the silver globe hanging suspended above the ocean.

"Strangely enough—" a furrow made a vertical crease between his brows "—I think I would find the house empty if you left."

His statement hovered in the air, electrifying her. She had difficulty trying to breathe and there was an odd fluttering in the pit of her stomach.

The hand on her shoulder began, almost impercepti-
bly, to exert pressure to draw her closer as his gaze slid
to her lips. Caught in his spell, it didn't occur to her to
resist, although Cole gave her the opportunity. His
boldly defined mouth slowly descended to hers.

With a firmness absent of demand, he explored every
curve of her full, soft lips. His hand lay along the side of
her neck, his thumb resting against the tiny pulse that
was racing madly. The blood tingled through her veins,
setting every nerve alert.

He lifted his head a fraction of an inch, the scent of
tobacco in the warm breath that caressed her skin.
"Strawberry, isn't it?" he murmured huskily.

"What?" Lacey opened her eyes weakly and was
immediately overcome by the sensation that she could
drown in his indigo eyes.

"Your lipstick. It's strawberry, isn't it?" Cole repeated softly, and tasted her trembling lower lip.

"Yes," she whispered, and unconsciously swayed
toward him.

"I always did have a weakness for strawberry." It
was an absent comment. Lacey doubted if Cole was
aware that he had said it aloud.

Then his mouth opened moistly over hers, devouring
its ripeness as his strong fingers curled into the back of
her neck, tilting her head backward to more fully receive
his burning kiss. His other arm reached for her waist
and Lacey pliantly let herself be arched against his hard,
muscled length.

With consumate skill, Cole demanded a response and
she gave it quite naturally. Her fingers spread over his
chest to slide around his neck into the thickness of his

dark hair. A melting sensuality seemed to flow through her limbs as his mouth faultlessly continued its task of arousal until her hunger became an exquisite pain.

The light breeze from the ocean cooled her heated skin, but it couldn't abate the molten fire spreading through her veins. His experience far outstripped hers and she gloried in it, finding a heady exultation in the heights of abandoned passion.

The embrace that had begun so slowly ended abruptly with Cole pushing her an arm's length away. Dazed by the unexpected rejection, Lacey looked at him with inviting, luminously brown eyes. She could hear his ragged breathing and quivered at the sound.

A pained yet wry smile crooked his mouth. "You'll have to forgive me for that, Lacey." His voice was low and roughly controlled.

"Yes...." But it was more of a question than it was an answer.

"You're a potent little package and more vulnerable than I realized," he added, exhaling a long breath.

"So are you," she admitted shakily, still confused. "But I don't see why you should apologize for kissing me. I may have said I was old-fashioned, but I'm not a prude."

"I wish you were." Cole smiled ruefully.

"That's an odd thing to say," Lacey murmured. He wasn't making any sense to her.

"Is it?" He let go of her arms and she had to stand without his support. Her knees trembled for an instant before they found the necessary strength.

"I think it is," she insisted.

"Our agreement isn't even twenty-four hours old and

I was on the verge of breaking one of our first ground rules," Cole stated in a mocking tone. "No sex."

Crimson flamed through her cheeks and just as quickly burned itself out, leaving her complexion unnaturally pale as she acknowledged the truth of his observation. She had lost control of herself for a moment.

There was no telling for certain just how far she might have let Cole go before she came to her senses. It was a sobering discovery.

He watched her changing color for a silent minute before he smiled gently. "Good night, Lacey." Turning on his heel, he walked into the house.

"Good night," Lacey echoed him faintly, and doubted if her voice had been strong enough to carry into the house to him.

She pivoted back to the ocean view, shivering at the sudden chill that danced over her arms. The fires inside of her were slowly being brought under control.

She remembered Cole's saying that the situation between them wouldn't get out of hand unless they permitted it. They had both come dangerously close to it. Cole had been the first to realize it, but it was just hitting Lacey now.

# CHAPTER FIVE

THE BUZZ of the alarm clock hammered at her eardrums, and with a groan, Lacey rolled onto her side. She must have set the clock last night out of habit.

Her fumbling hand reached out for the knob to switch it off, only to discover the alarm wasn't turned on. Still the buzzing sound continued to drone its wake-up call.

Frowning, Lacey forced her eyes open. It was several seconds before she realized that the sound was coming from Cole's bedroom. It was his alarm clock she was hearing. She grabbed the second pillow and crushed it over her ears, trying to drown out the sound, but it continued with monotonous persistence.

"Oh, why don't you wake up and turn that darn thing off?" she moaned into the pillow. But the buzzing didn't stop. "I'll never get back to sleep!"

Angrily she tossed the pillow away and stumbled out of bed. She walked over to pound on the bedroom wall, remembering too late that the bathroom was between the two guest rooms. Grabbing her housecoat, she shrugged into it as she stalked into the hallway to Cole's door.

She hammered on it with her fist. "Shut that alarm off!" It kept right on buzzing. "Cole!"

There was an answering squeak of the bedsprings, then blissful silence. Sighing, Lacey hurried back into her own room and crawled under the covers, housecoat and all. As she closed her eyes, she heard his door open and the firm padding of his bare feet in the hall.

The bathroom door opened and closed. A few seconds later the shower was turned on full force, the hammering of its spray sounding as loud and as nerve-racking as the alarm clock.

"I want to go to sleep," Lacey moaned in self-pity.

Within a few short minutes, another sound joined that of the rushing water in the shower. "Oh, no," she groaned, "he isn't!" She listened. "He *is*. He's singing in the shower. That does it!"

The bedclothes were thrown aside again. It was absolutely pointless to try to go back to sleep now. She stalked angrily into the kitchen, opening and slamming the refrigerator door to get some orange juice and repeating the procedure when she put it back.

While she sipped at her juice, she readied the percolator to make coffee, perversely hoping that when she filled the pot with cold water, Cole would get scalded with hot water in the shower. After plugging the pot in, she hopped onto the tall stool at the kitchen's counter bar.

A quarter of an hour later, the coffee pot was emitting its last sighing pop when Cole walked in from the living room. A cigarette was dangling from his mouth while his hands were completing the knot of his tie. He saw Lacey sitting at the counter and frowned.

"I thought you were going to sleep late this morning," he said. "What are you doing up?"

"It takes gall to ask that question," Lacey declared with an exasperated look.

Cole grimaced with mocking ruefulness. "My alarm clock woke you up, did it?"

"Your alarm clock, followed by the shower and your stunning serenade," she answered caustically, enumerating the causes.

He paused beside the counter to rest his cigarette in the ashtray. There was a roguish glint in his blue eyes. "The strawberry is green and tart this morning, isn't it?"

"You would be, too, if it were the other way around." But her tone was less sharp.

"Is there any juice?"

"In the refrigerator. And there's coffee made, too," Lacey added.

He glanced at her empty juice glass. "Shall I pour you a cup of coffee?" he asked as he walked around the counter.

"Might as well," she sighed. After all, she was already awake and the freshly perked coffee had a decidedly pleasing aroma.

First Cole poured himself a small glass of orange juice from the refrigerator and downed it before taking two cups from the cupboard. He filled them and set them side by side on the counter, then walked around it to join Lacey.

He fingered the knot of his tie and muttered, "It isn't straight, is it?"

"No," Lacey admitted. When he started to try to redo it by touch alone, she said, "Here, let me." Cole didn't argue.

When she was finished, he inspected it with his hand, his eyebrow twisting in surprised approval. "That's very good. Where did you learn that?"

"I have a father and two brothers," she answered. "And they're all thumbs when it comes to tying ties."

"No sisters?" Cole sipped at his coffee, seemingly impervious to its burning temperature.

"None. Your cigarette is in the ashtray," she reminded him as the smoke wafted into her eyes.

He reached over and snubbed it out. "I have two sisters, both married and each with her own brood of little ones." He took another drink of his coffee.

"Neither of my brothers is married yet." Lacey tried her coffee and decided to wait until it had cooled more.

"Your parents must be getting anxious for grandchildren."

"I don't know. . . ." She smiled faintly. "My mother claims she's too young to be a grandmother. She certainly looks too young."

Cole glanced at the gold watch on his wrist and gulped down the rest of his coffee. "I'm late," he declared grimly.

Hesitating beside her stool, he crooked a finger under her chin. "I'm sorry for waking you up this morning."

The devastating smile he gave her was Lacey's undoing. She found she could not summon any anger at the way he had deprived her of a few extra hours' sleep. But she wouldn't go so far as to admit that.

"I suppose I shouldn't get into the habit of sleeping late anyway," she said instead.

Before she could guess his intention, he bent down

and kissed her firmly. "You know this could become a habit?" A dancing light twinkled in his eyes.

Lacey wished her heart would stop beating so erratically. "You're forgetting the ground rules," she pointed out tersely.

"Oh?" Cole said it as if he'd forgotten about them, but the gleam in his eyes said differently. "That's right, I had."

The house seemed empty when he left.

IT WAS EIGHT-THIRTY-ONE that evening when Cole's car drove into the garage. Lacey knew exactly because she had been glancing at the clock nearly every five minutes since seven. But she steeled herself to react calmly and casually when he entered the living room. He looked haggard and exhausted, his briefcase in hand.

"Rough day?" Lacey questioned with pretended idleness. She glanced up from the fashion magazine she was supposedly reading.

"More or less," he nodded, and sat down in the other sofa.

"Have you eaten?"

"What?" Cole looked at her blankly before her question registered. "Oh, yes, I stopped on the way."

Lacey thought of the dinner she had kept warming in the oven after having eaten her portion, but said nothing. Cole opened his briefcase and took out a sheaf of legal-looking documents.

It was on the tip of Lacey's tongue to suggest that he should relax instead of doing more work, but she bit it into silence with a firm reminder that it was none of her business if he worked himself to death.

For all the notice he paid to her the rest of the evening, she could have been another throw pillow on the sofa. She tried to convince herself that she didn't care, but she knew it wasn't true.

Finally, at half-past ten, she tossed the magazine onto the table and rose. Cole glanced up with a questioning frown.

"It's late. I'm going to turn in," she said stiffly. "Good night."

"Good night," he returned indifferently, and looked back at his papers.

Pressing her lips tightly together, Lacey pivoted sharply. Tears were stinging her eyes and there was a bitter taste in her mouth.

"Oh, by the way," Cole spoke up and she glanced quickly back to him, "the toilets showed up today."

"They did?"

"It seems they've been in the city for the last two weeks—at the wrong warehouse," he replied with thinly disguised impatience. "It's a pity no one bothered to check on them before."

Anger simmered near the surface as Lacey read implied criticism of her in the comment, but Cole's attention was again riveted to his papers. She checked her biting reply, wondering if he even remembered that she worked for Mike Bowman. Holding her head stiffly erect, she walked down the hallway to her bedroom.

THE NEXT TWO DAYS were a repeat of Monday, with Lacey waking at the buzz of Cole's alarm and Cole returning late in the evening to bury himself in paperwork. Except for the early mornings and late evenings,

Lacey could have been staying at the house by herself, since she was either alone or left alone.

In the mornings she filled her time swimming in the ocean and strolling on the beach. The afternoons she would relax on the shaded balcony and read. Meals were a haphazard affair. She didn't repeat the mistake of the first night by keeping food warm for Cole. Lacey tried not to admit it, but her days were spent waiting for Cole to return.

On Thursday evening she went to bed as usual some time after ten, leaving Cole in the living room with his papers. She fell asleep almost instantly, but it was a restless, fitful sleep that finally wakened her shortly after midnight.

Her mouth was all woolly and dry. She slid out of bed and padded sleepily to her door. As she opened it, the artificial light glared harshly to momentarily blind her.

Shielding her eyes with her hand, she started to grope for the switch to turn off the hall light that Cole had left burning, but the whisper of papers being shuffled in the living room halted her hand.

She walked into the living room, her bare feet making little sound, her eyes still squinting at the unaccustomed light. Cole was sitting on the sofa where she had left him hours ago, going over his papers and making voluminous notes on a long yellow tablet.

"Haven't you gone to bed yet?" she demanded accusingly in a voice husky with sleep. "It's after midnight."

Cole glanced up sharply, momentarily startled out of his concentrations. One eyebrow twisted into a frown as he looked from Lacey to the gold watch gleaming below the rolled-up cuff of his white sleeve. His mouth thinned briefly before he bent over his papers again.

"I'm almost done," he stated, then asked absently, "What are you doing up?"

"I was thirsty," she retorted, and resumed her path to the kitchen, doubting that he had even heard her answer.

As she passed by the sofa, Cole rubbed the back of his neck and arched his shoulders in a tired stretch. "Damn, but I'm tired," he murmured to no one in particular.

"You could go to bed," she called back to him as she entered the kitchen, walked to the sink, and turned on the cold water tap. Perversely, she didn't feel any sympathy for him. If he was tired, the solution was simple. Since he didn't choose to make it, she wasn't going to waste words feeling sorry for him.

"I have to get this done."

Opening the cupboard door, she took out a glass. "Didn't you ever read *Gone with the Wind*? 'Tomorrow is another day.'"

"I need to have this first thing in the morning," he answered curtly.

"I suppose the world will come to an end if you don't," Lacey taunted.

After filling the glass with water, she started to raise it to her lips and, turning slightly, discovered that Cole had followed her into the kitchen. The tiredly etched corners of his mouth twisted briefly into a smile at her gibe, but he made no reply to it.

"Is there any coffee?" he asked instead.

She glanced at the percolator, noticing the cord unplugged from the socket. "If there is, it's cold."

"We have instant coffee, don't we?" Cole opened the cupboard door nearest him.

"In here." She gestured to the cupboard above her head without offering to get it for him.

Lacey did move to one side to avoid getting banged in the head when he opened it. Sipping at her water, she watched him take the jar down and spoon some dark crystals into a cup.

She became fascinated by his hands, strong and tanned, and the scattering of bronze hair curling on the portion of his arm exposed by the rolled-up sleeve. Her pulse fluttered, faintly disturbed. She took a quick swallow of water in an effort to forget his unsettling nearness.

"Aren't you going to heat some water?" she chided, certain he had overlooked it in his tiredness.

"It would take too much time." He stepped around her to turn on the tap. "The hot water from the tap will be good enough."

He let the water run until steam was rising from the sink, then ran it in his cup to fill it. He leaned a hip against the counter near Lacey as if too tired to support himself. Brushing a hand over his mouth and chin, he reached for a spoon to stir his coffee, but it slipped out of his fingers and clattered to the tiled floor.

As she stooped quickly to retrieve it, Lacey's fingers touched the handle at the same time that Cole took hold of the curve of the spoon.

They straightened together, each holding onto the spoon, an elemental tension coursing through Lacey. There was a velvet quality to the midnight blue of his eyes that did little to slow the sudden acceleration of her pulse.

"That was clumsy of me," he chided himself, and Lacey released her hold on the spoon.

"You're tired." She forced an evenness into her voice. "You should come to bed."

"Is that an invitation?" Despite the husky amusement running through his voice, there was a thread of seriousness that rocketed Lacey's heart into her throat.

"You know what I meant." She swirled the water in her glass and took a quick swallow.

"Mmmm."

She didn't know whether that meant yes or no, and glanced at Cole for a clearer answer. There was an unnerving darkness in the look he was giving her. It roamed over her face, touching the sleek fur-brown cap of her hair, the wing of an eyebrow, the finely chiseled bone of her cheek and the soft curve of her lips.

His wandering gaze didn't stop there, but traveled leisurely down the slender column of her golden-tanned neck to dwell on the rounded curve of her breasts. They seemed to swell under the almost physical caress of his eyes, the rosy peaks thrusting against the silklike material of her pajamas.

The sensations he was arousing inside her were both sensuous and seductive. She was possessed by the dangerous urge to glide into his arms and mold her supple body against his hard, rangy length.

Alarm bells rang a warning inside her head as his gaze began to slide down her stomach, starting a delicious curling sensation in her loins.

"Cole, stop it!" she protested shakily.

His answer was to move in front of Lacey, an arm braced on the counter on either side of her, trapping

her. A traitorous weakness caused her knees to tremble.
She felt giddily light-headed, a feeling that increased as
the rippling muscles of his legs pressed against her
thighs.

Bending his head, he sought the curve of her neck,
teasing the sensitive skin with his mouth. And the caress
carried a promise of something more. Lacey quivered in
expectation. He nibbled moistly on her neck, his breath
warm against her skin.

"I want you, Lacey," he murmured against her
throat.

When he put into words what had only been a nebu-
lous thought in her mind, she wakened to the danger of
the moment. Regardless of how strong his attraction
was, she wouldn't be any man's plaything—to be used
and discarded when his amusement was over. And Cole
was capable of that. Hadn't he virtually ignored her for
the past four days?

One minute she was pliantly yielding to his touch and
the next she was ducking under his arms and stepping
quickly away. He turned slowly, almost in surprise, as if
he hadn't realized she could slip away, nor that she
would want to.

"You were forgetting the ground rules again, Cole,"
she reminded him, her voice breathless. "Besides, you
have your paperwork to finish." She retreated a step
under his direct stare. "And your coffee is getting cold,
too."

Cole made no move toward her and she turned to
hurry to her bedroom, tossing hastily over her shoulder,
"Good night."

As she started to close her door, Cole's quiet voice

carried from the living room, taunting softly, "You were forgetting the ground rules, too, Lacey."

There wasn't any reply she could make to that.

YELLOW BEAMS OF SUNLIGHT peeped through the slit of the curtains. Lacey opened an eye, absently studying the dancing particles of dust caught in the sliver of light.

Lifting her head from the pillow, she glanced at the clock and groaned. It was six o'clock. Obviously she had wakened in anticipation of Cole's alarm going off. She covered her head with the pillow and waited for the customary buzz.

Ten minutes later there was still no sound of the alarm clock going off. Not that it mattered, she sighed. She couldn't go back to sleep even if Cole had decided to have a late morning after working so late last night.

Climbing out of bed, she put on her housecoat and walked out the door into the hall. The door to Cole's bedroom stood open, and automatically she glanced inside as she tiptoed by. The bed was made.

"That's a first!" Lacey murmured wryly. Usually she made his bed after he had left in the morning.

Either Cole had risen much earlier or else he hadn't bothered to go to bed at all. He had still been in the living room working when she had finally gone back to sleep. It was possible that when he finished, he had dressed and gone into the office early. Or. . . .

Lacey tiptoed into the living room. There he was, half sitting and half lying on the sofa, fully dressed, with his papers and notes strewn on the cushions around him. He looked so tired that she disliked the thought of waking him. But he also looked very uncomfortable.

As quietly as she could, she gathered up the papers scattered around him and set them in neat stacks on the lid of his briefcase. She managed to slip one of the throw pillows beneath his head and was debating whether she could swing his legs onto the cushions without waking him.

He stirred and she became motionless. Sleepy dark blue eyes peered at her through a screen of dark spiky lashes. Cole shifted slightly and grimaced, as if cramped muscles were making their soreness known.

"What time is it?" he mumbled.

"About a quarter past six."

Groaning, he rubbed his forehead. "It can't be. I was only going to rest my eyes for a few minutes."

"From the looks of you, you could do with a few more minutes of 'rest,'" Lacey suggested dryly.

"I can't." He pushed himself into a sitting position, arching his back and watching. "I have a meeting first thing this morning. I have to get into the office."

There was no use arguing; he wouldn't listen to her anyway. "I'll put some coffee on," she said instead.

She did just that while Cole showered and changed. A glass of orange juice was sitting on the counter for him when he entered the kitchen. She assured herself that she had only done it because she felt sorry for him.

"That helped," he declared after downing the juice.

Maybe, Lacey conceded to herself, but the reviving effect of the juice would be short-lived. Even after showering and putting on fresh clothes, there were still lines of strain and weariness cracking the vital mask.

"You really should get more rest, Cole," she said impulsively. "Get some sleep instead of working all night."

"The work has to be done." He shrugged and walked to the sink counter to set down the glass and pour a cup of coffee.

"You should do it at your office and not bring so much home at night," Lacey retorted.

"I get ten times as much done here as I ever did at the office. There aren't any distractions or interruptions." Cole paused, glancing at her. "Or at least, there aren't as many distractions."

Lacey pretended not to understand that comment. "It's no skin off my nose if you work yourself to death," she retorted stepping down from the bar stool.

"Where are you going?" He eyed her curiously.

"To shower and dress." She started into the living room.

"Lacey?" She paused to look at him. "Thanks for waking me up," Cole said, smiling.

Returning his smile, Lacey nodded and quickened her steps to the hall. He was gone by the time she had finished showering.

The previous days of her vacation had seemed to pass swiftly, but today the hours were dragging. It was barely the middle of the afternoon and she felt completely at a loose end. She had lain in the sun for as long as she dared, then sought the shade of the balcony, stretching out on a lounge chair with a book. But it had failed to hold her interest.

Sighing, she slid a piece of paper between the pages to mark her place and set it down. She stood up and walked to the railing, lifting her face to the cooling breeze blowing from the ocean.

She was still wearing her shiny one-piece bathing suit,

an unusual blue gray color. Maybe she could change her clothes and drive into Virginia Beach to treat herself to a dinner out.

The ring of the doorbell resounded distantly through the house. She turned in surprise, wondering who would be calling at this hour of a Friday afternoon. All of her close friends were working. Of course, there was always the possibility that it was a salesman.

Any distraction was welcome, so she went to answer the door, hurrying into the house to glide swiftly down the stairs. She peered through the peephole and frowned. It looked like Mike standing outside. She opened the door and confirmed the identification.

"I was hoping you'd be here," he announced with a smile.

"You should be working!" It was almost an accusation.

"I should be," Mike agreed, stepping into the house as Lacey moved aside to admit him. "But it's been one long, hectic week and I told the bosses I was taking off early today. And if they didn't like it, they could shove it."

"It's been as bad as that, has it?" Lacey grinned, knowing that Mike would never have put it that bluntly in his request.

She had been uneasy about meeting Mike again after that disastrous dinner. But within seconds after opening the door, she found that his attitude allowed her to slip back into the comfortable relationship they had previously shared. It made her feel good that the breach between them had been repaired.

"Worse!" he exclaimed with mock exaggeration.

"How far will a cold beer go to making it worth-while?" she teased.

"It sounds better than a paycheck right now," Mike laughed. "Just lead me to it."

"Follow me," said Lacey, ascending the steps. "I know there's at least a couple of cans in the refrigerator."

A few minutes later, ensconced in a lounge chair on the balcony with a cold beer in his hand, Mike declared with a long sigh of contentment, "Now, this is living. Peace and quiet and your own unobstructed view of the ocean. I kept thinking about this view all week."

"And all the while, I've been thinking you'd driven all the way out here to see me," Lacey sighed mockingly.

"Oh, I did," he assured her, settling deeper into his chair. "I never realized what a gem of a secretary I had until you went on vacation."

"How is Donna doing?"

"She's driving me up the wall—that's how she's doing," Mike grumbled.

"She really is a very competent secretary." Lacey defended her co-worker while offering a wry smile of understanding.

"She is, yes," he agreed. "But she chatters like a magpie all day long, saying the dumbest things. I can't make up my mind if all that naiveté is for real or if it's an act she puts on because she thinks it's cute."

"I'm afraid the bulk of it is genuine."

"Thank God it's only another week before you come back." Mike took a swig of his beer. "More than that and I think I'd hand in my resignation."

"Really?" A mischievous light twinkled in her brown eyes. "I was thinking of giving you a two-week notice and recommending Donna to take my place permanently."

She squealed with laughter as Mike came bounding out of his chair, catching her by the wrist. Gaining a firmer hold, he swept her into his arms and off her feet to hold her over the balcony railing.

"Put me down, Mike!" She was laughing so hard she could hardly talk, her fingers clinging to his arms instinctively rather than out of fear.

"Take back what you said or so help me, I'll drop you!" he threatened, but his dancing hazel eyes indicated that he had not the slightest intention of carrying it out.

# CHAPTER SIX

"I TAKE IT BACK! I take it back!" Lacey promised between gasps of breathless laughter.

Mike swung her away from the railing, letting her feet slide to the floor. "Don't ever joke about a thing like that again," he warned with a broad grin.

"I won't, believe me," she declared, leaning a shoulder heavily against his chest as she struggled to catch her breath.

"You'd better—"

"Is this where you go, Bowman, when you tell your office that you're out on a job site?" Cole's biting question wiped the smiles from both their faces.

Lacey turned with a jerk to see him standing in the doorway, the knot of his tie loosened and the top button of his shirt unfastened. He looked as tired and irritable as he had sounded, and coldly angry.

"The office was aware that I was through for the day when I left there an hour ago," Mike replied with commendable calm.

"That isn't what your secretary said," Cole snapped, his eyes glinting with the metallic blue of finely honed steel.

"Donna again!" Mike muttered beneath his breath.

And Lacey guessed that her replacement had decided

it was more politic to tell a client that Mike was working than that he had left early.

"It was an unwise decision on the part of Mike's temporary secretary to tell you that instead of the truth," she stated in Mike's defense.

"So you're playing the dutiful secretary again, rushing in to defend your boss," Cole taunted.

The angle of her chin increased. "I'm merely trying to straighten out your facts!" she retorted.

"Are you?" His mouth twisted cynically.

"And while we are on the subject of working, what are you doing here, Cole? Why aren't you at your office?" Lacey demanded accusingly.

"In case you've forgotten," he snapped, "I was up practically all night working!"

"So you decided to leave early," she concluded, and tipped her head to challenge him. "Can you be sure your secretary is telling that to those who call for you? Or will she make up some other excuse for your absence, the way Mike's secretary did when you called?"

"It sounds very plausible." Cole's voice was riddled with skepticism.

"The truth generally does," Lacey flashed.

His wintry steel eyes raked her from head to toe, taking in the shiny bathing suit that so attractively showed off her curves. "But I can't help wondering how many times this past week Bowman has been here when he was supposedly at a job site." On the last word, Cole pivoted sharply and walked away.

The arrogant set of his wide shoulders was like a red cape to a bull, and Lacey started to charge blindly after him. Mike laid a restraining hand on her arm.

"Let it be, Lacey," he suggested, recognizing the warning signs that her temper was ready to let fly.

She jerked her arm away from his hand and stalked into the house after Cole, catching up with him in the living room. In the act of stripping the tie from around his neck, Cole glanced at her coolly.

Lacey unleashed her anger in a flurry of acid words. "It's none of your business how many times Mike has been here this last week, *if* he's been here at all! Furthermore, he's my guest and—"

"Perhaps," Cole interrupted sharply, "if you'd possessed the common courtesy to let me know you were going to entertain tonight, I could have made other arrangements to be elsewhere so the two of you could be alone."

"So now you're accusing me of a lack of courtesy?" Her hands rested on her hips, fury trembling in her voice. "What about yours?"

"Mine? Because I was rude to Bowman, I suppose?" he concluded with a contemptuous twist of his mouth.

"Among other things," Lacey agreed.

He drew his head back to study her arrogantly. "What other things?" he demanded.

"Every single day this week your alarm has woken me up while you slept right through it," she retorted.

Lacey knew she was being goaded into this argument by more than just the things Cole had said against Mike. Some sort of an explosion had been building inside her all week. It had needed only a spark to ignite the fuse.

"I've apologized for that," Cole reminded her grimly.

"Apologies don't help me go back to sleep." Sarcasm licked her words.

"If you don't like our arrangement, why don't you move out?" he challenged.

"I am not moving out! You leave!" Lacey countered angrily.

"Why? So Bowman can move in? That would be cozy, wouldn't it?"

Lacey sputtered impotently for a second. "His company would certainly be preferable to yours!"

"I bet it would. No ground rules. No separate bedrooms. No separate beds." Cole snapped out the words almost savagely.

"Your mind is as dirty and vile as your words are!" Lacey flashed spitefully. "You should marry Monica. You're two of a kind!"

"I'm leaving," Mike declared from the balcony door. "I didn't come here to start a free-for-all."

Lacey turned with a start. For a few minutes she had forgotten Mike was even there. "Don't go, Mike. Cole was just leaving," she insisted tightly.

"Like hell I am!" he growled. "You can either do your entertaining while I'm in the house or go somewhere else. But I am not leaving."

"Fine." Lacey clipped out the word and glanced at Mike. "Give me a couple of minutes to get dressed and I'll go with you."

He gave her a brief nod of agreement and Lacey walked purposefully to her room. Stripping off her bathing suit, she hurriedly donned her undergarments and an apricot flowered sundress. A taut silence stretched from the living room, its oppressive stillness spreading through all the rooms.

Mike was waiting at the head of the stairs when she

reappeared. Skirting the grim-visaged Cole, she walked to the staircase to join Mike. He shifted uncomfortably as Lacey paused to cast a fiery look at Cole.

"The house is yours for the evening," she told him with a cloying smile. "You can have all the peace and quiet you've been wanting." The sweetness turned to venom as she added, "And I hope it smothers you!"

With a toss of her head, she swept past Mike down the steps to the front door. Outside, the staccato click of her sandal heels on the pavement indicated that her anger had not fully abated. Mike moved forward to walk beside her, lengthening his stride to keep up with her rapid pace.

"Considering the present circumstances, Lacey," he began hesitantly, "don't you think it would be better if you moved back to your apartment for the rest of your vacation?"

"And let that man win?" she flashed. "Not on your life! I wouldn't give him that satisfaction. I can make his life as miserable as he makes mine."

Stopping beside his car, she waited expectantly for him to open the door for her. When he didn't immediately, she glanced at him and noticed the rather pained expression on his face.

"What's wrong, Mike?" she demanded, the crispness of leftover anger still in her voice.

"I don't know how to tell you this," he murmured uncomfortably.

"Tell me what?" Her patience was in short supply.

His gaze ricocheted away from hers. "I have a date tonight," he announced flatly.

"You have a *what*?" Of all the ironies, that had to be

the tops! Lacey nearly chocked on a gurgle of bitter laughter.

"I'm sorry, Lacey," he offered grimly. "I thought I'd stop over for a couple of hours to relax and talk, then get out before Whitfield came."

And she had automatically assumed that he had arrived for the evening. That definitely had to be the height of self-conceit, whether she had been aware of it or not.

She glanced back at the house. She simply could not go back there, not until much later. Cole would never let her hear the end of it if he learned the truth.

"It's all right, Mike," she said finally. "It's just what I deserve."

"What are you going to do?"

"I'm not going back in there and have Cole start gloating, that's for sure," she declared emphatically. "I'll go somewhere. Would you mind waiting a couple of minutes while I get my car out of the garage?"

"Of course I'll wait," Mike promised, smiling that it was the least he could do after letting her down.

Lacey hoped it would look to Cole as if they were going somewhere together but in separate vehicles. As she backed her car out of the garage, she glanced up to the second-story window looking out from the living room and saw Cole gazing out of it.

A surge of anger washed through her and she reversed recklessly out of the driveway without looking for traffic. Immediately she shifted gears, and pressed the accelerator to the floor, the tires peeling rubber as the car shot forward, leaving Mike far behind.

At the major highway intersection, Mike finally

caught up with her. His honking horn made Lacey glance in her rearview mirror to see him motioning her onto the shoulder of the road. Grimly she pulled over. He parked behind her and climbed out of his car to walk to hers.

Mike bent down to peer in her open window. "Who the hell do you think you are? A race driver?"

"Is that why you stopped me? Just to criticize my driving?" Lacey challenged, in no mood for a lecture.

"No...although it's a damned good reason for stopping you." He didn't back down completely from his stand. "It's just that...I feel responsible for what happened back there. Your whole argument with Whitfield started because you were defending me, whether I asked you to or not."

"The argument was inevitable." Her fingers drummed the steering wheel. Lacey was impatient to be on her way, even if she didn't know where she was going.

"I put you in an awkward position. I should have told you when I first arrived that I had a date with someone else tonight." Mike gallantly took the blame for her present dilemma.

"It isn't your fault," Lacey denied. "I was the one who put my foot in my mouth. I didn't need help from anyone to do that."

"What are you going to do tonight?" His look was sympathetic and compassionate.

"I don't know." Her gaze skittered away from his face.

"I don't like the idea of your being alone. I could round up one of my friends and make a foursome," he suggested.

"I'd be rotten company for anyone, but thanks. Besides I wouldn't want to cramp your style." She attempted a smile, but it wasn't very successful.

"What are you going to do, Lacey? You can't just drive around all night."

She hesitated before answering. "Maybe I'll stop by to see Maryann."

Her statement seemed to satisfy Mike. "You do that. And drive carefully, will you, Lacey?"

"I promise." As Mike straightened, Lacey shifted her car into gear.

She checked for oncoming vehicles before pulling into the traffic lane, waving to Mike. Obeying the speed limits, she drove sensibly to the apartment complex where Maryann lived. She parked her car in the visitors' lot and walked up the steps to her friend's unit. Lacey rang the doorbell and waited.

The door, still secured by a chain latch, opened a crack. Through the narrow opening, Lacey glimpsed the washed-out brown hair, that peculiar dark blond shade, so distinctively Maryann's.

"Hi. It's me, Lacey," she identified herself to her cautious friend.

"Lacey, what are you doing here?" The door closed a moment, then swung wide to admit her. "I thought you'd be having your own private little clambake on the beach tonight."

"My own clambake, huh?" Lacey's smile was twisted. "And I came to see if you had a hot dog to share." As she walked in, she noticed that her girl friend was wearing a housecoat. Only then did it occur to her that it was Friday night and it was very likely her friend had a date. "I bet you're going out, aren't you?"

"No, it's just another Friday night for me and my cat to spend together. I was just changing out of the clothes I wore to work when you rang the doorbell. Both of us will be glad to have you for dinner," Maryann insisted as a pumpkin-colored cat sauntered from the kitchen to rub against his mistress's leg. "I don't have any hot dogs, but I do have some hamburger."

"That's fine." Lacey really didn't have any appetite.

Maryann closed the door, locked it and refastened the chain. "You never did say what you're doing here. Did it get too lonely out there in your luxurious beach house?"

"No, it wasn't lonely. Far from it," Lacey declared.

"What do you mean?" Maryann frowned. "I thought you didn't have any close neighbors."

"It's a long story," was the sighing answer.

"I have all night if you do." Her friend shrugged away that excuse.

"It isn't lonely because I'm not staying in the house by myself," announced Laccy.

"You're not staying in the house alone." Maryann repeated the statement to be certain she had understood it. "That means someone is staying with you. Who?"

"Cole Whitfield."

"Who is Cole Whitfield?" Almost immediately a light dawned in her eyes. "Whitfield? You don't mean the sarcastic Mr. Whitfield?"

"That is precisely the Cole Whitfield that I mean."

Maryann's mouth opened in astonishment. For several seconds, she was incapable of getting any words to come out. Finally she managed to ask, "How? What is he doing there?"

"It seems that Cole is an old family friend of Margo's husband. There was a mix-up. Margo asked me to stay at the house and her husband asked Cole."

"But when you found out...."

"It's all totally unbelievable, Maryann. I thought he was a burglar when he first walked into the house. He scared me out of my wits." Lacey went on to explain how she and Cole had come to the agreement to share the house.

"And you actually agreed, after the things you said about him?" Maryann was incredulous.

"In person, he really isn't so bad. What am I saying?" Lacey caught herself angrily. "He's worse. His alarm wakes me up in the morning. He sings in the shower. He works till all hours of the night, then is grouchy as an old bear."

"Lacey—" Maryann gave her a long, considering look "—maybe you should tell me something about this Cole Whitfield. Like, for instance, how old is he and what does he look like?"

"He's in his thirties," she admitted.

"Unmarried," Maryann inserted with certainty.

"Yes, unmarried," she nodded.

"Good-looking?"

"In a rough kind of way. He has nice blue eyes, though."

"And all you are doing is sharing the same house." Her friend eyed her skeptically. "There haven't been any 'romantic' moments between you?"

"I don't know what you mean by romantic. I sleep in my room and he sleeps in his."

"And he hasn't made a single pass at you?" Maryann took one look at Lacey's face and had her answer.

Lacey didn't try to conceal what she felt any longer. "It's all a mess. I'm half in love with him already. Lord knows he doesn't give me much encouragement."

"What happened tonight? Does he have a date with someone else? Is that why you've come here? To show him that he isn't the only pebble on the beach?"

"He doesn't have a date. He came home to have an early night." Lacey was unaware that she had referred to the beach house as home, but that was what it had become to her since she had started sharing it with Cole. "Mike was there. He'd stopped by for a beer. Cole got all hostile because he had called the office and Donna had told him Mike was working at another job site instead of explaining he had left early today. We started arguing and the whole thing became personal."

"You lost your temper and stormed out of the house," Maryann finished for her.

"Cole thinks I'm going out with Mike tonight. And Mike already has a date," Lacey explained.

"When did you find this out?"

"After I had stormed out of the house," she admitted with chagrin. Instantly her chin lifted to a defiant angle. "I couldn't go back then and endure Cole's gloating."

"So you came here."

"I didn't know where else to go." Lacey shrugged and glanced apologetically at the dark blonde girl.

"What are friends for?" Maryann smiled. "Come on. Let's fix a salad, fry some hamburgers and have some wine."

Lacey hesitated for only a second. "I'll fix the salad."

After their meal, they sat around Maryann's small living room, talking and listening to records. A little after eleven, Lacey saw Maryann stifling a yawn.

"I'm sorry. I forgot you have to work tomorrow morning, don't you?" Lacey remembered. "I'd better leave so you can get some sleep."

"You don't have to go," Maryann protested, rising to her feet when Lacey did.

"It's late. I think it's safe for me to go back now," she joked weakly.

"Call me and let me know what happens," her friend urged, then clicked her tongue. "I forgot. You don't have a phone out there."

"No, but I'll have lunch with you one day this next week and give you the blow-by-blow details. If there are any," she laughed. "More than likely Cole is in bed and won't have any idea what time I get in. Or care what time it is."

"You can always make a lot of noise and wake him up when you come in," Maryann suggested with a conspiring laugh.

"Cole sleeps through his alarm. I think he'd sleep through an atom-bomb explosion." Lacey started for the door. "Thanks for dinner...and the company."

"It was fun." She reached down to pick up her cat. "Wasn't it, Oscar?" The cat purred and rubbed its head against her chin.

"Good night." Lacey was smiling as she left the apartment.

Once outside in the pleasant coolness of the night air, her expression sobered. She wasn't ready to return to the beach house yet. In her car, Lacey drove aimlessly through the streets. Finally she ended up on the Virginia Beach side of the bay along the ocean front.

Disregarding the lateness of the hour, she parked her

car and strolled along the silent beach. The time she had spent with her friend had been good, but Lacey still felt depressed. Finally the cool breeze drove her back to the car and she headed homeward.

*All in all not the best evening I've ever spent, but thanks to Maryann, not the worst,* Lacey thought as she drove the car into the garage. She had left her watch on the bedroom dresser and the clock on the car's dash didn't work. She had no idea what time it was. She knew it was late because it had been dark for hours.

Shivering at the coolness of the night air, she hurried through the connecting door from the garage to the house entrance. Wearily she began the tedious climb up the stairs.

Three steps from the top, the back of her neck prickled in warning and she glanced up to see Cole towering above her at the head of the stairs.

His white shirt was completely unbuttoned and pulled free of the waistband of his pants to hang loosely open. There was a forbidding darkness to his gaze, his rugged male features appearing to be permanently cast in bronze.

"Where the hell have you been?" he snarled.

"That's none of your business." Lacey attempted to brush past him, but his fingers clamped themselves vise-like over her wrist to stop her.

"Do you have any idea what time it is?" Cole demanded harshly.

"No, I don't, and I don't see that it matters," she retorted.

"It happens to be nearly four o'clock in the morning," he informed her. "I want to know where you've been."

Lacey strained against the steel-hard grip on her wrist. "I don't have to account to you for my whereabouts. Let me go, if you please," she ordered curtly. "I'm tired."

"I'll let you go," Cole promised, "as soon as you tell me where you've been."

"I told you it's none of your business where I've been," she repeated. She was tired and ill-equipped to engage in a slanging match with Cole Whitfield.

"I know you weren't with Bowman," he snapped.

Lacey paled visibly but challenged, "Wasn't I?"

"No, you weren't," There wasn't a trace of uncertainty in his ironclad statement. "Because I went to his place to find you. Bowman told me you'd said you were in no mood for anyone's company and had left."

Silently Lacey thanked Mike for inventing a face-saving answer instead of admitting that he had had a date with some other girl that night. But it still didn't get her out of her present situation.

"And I'm still not in the mood for anyone's company—least of all yours! Now let me go!" She tried twisting her arm to free if from his grip.

But Cole used the movement to curve her arm behind her back and haul her against his chest. "I don't care whether you're in the mood for company or not. You're going to answer my questions," he ordered angrily.

"I am not!" Lacey protested vehemently.

His other hand raked through her hair, his fingers gripping the short strands to force her head back so he could see her face.

"You've been drinking, haven't you?" he accused.

"I stopped at a friend's house and had a couple of

glasses of wine," she answered truthfully. "Is that a crime?"

"Considering the way you drove when you left here, it borders on attempted suicide," Cole snapped. "I've called the police half a dozen times, certain you'd had an accident, especially after I discovered you weren't with Bowman."

"I didn't have an accident. I arrived safely." Tears were misting her eyes. "I seem to be more in danger of being hurt by you than in my car." And she meant that in more than one way. "Let go of my arm! You're going to break it if you keep twisting it like that."

"I hope it hurts." He forced her more fully against his rigid length. "After what you put me through tonight, you deserve to be punished."

"What I put you through?" Lacey choked in bitter laughter. "Why, you arrogant, bullheaded—"

Cole gave her no time to finish the insult. His mouth bruised her lips into silence as his arms ruthlessly molded her to his body with an economy of movement. Yet the cruel kiss meant to punish ignited a bewildering response in Lacey. She had meant to struggle, to fight his embrace, but her hands were sliding inside his shirt, seeking the fiery warmth of his naked skin. Her head was whirling, throbbing painfully, confused by her reaction.

When Cole lifted his head, she could not open her eyes to look at him, quivering with the response his kiss had evoked. She felt his mouth and chin rubbing against the hair near her forehead.

"For God's sake, Lacey, where were you all this time?" There was a funny throb in his voice, almost like pain, as his mouth moved against her hair while he spoke, roughly caressing. "I've been half out of my mind worrying that something had happened to you."

"Really?" she breathed, almost afraid to believe him.

"Yes, really." He smiled against her cheek and she felt the uneven thud of his heart beneath her hands. "Your friend, the one you had a drink with—" his arms tightened around her, demand creeping back into his voice "—was it a man or a woman?"

"It was Maryann, my girl friend," Lacey admitted, tipping her head to the side as he began nuzzling her ear.

"And I suppose you've been gossiping with her all night while I've been pacing the floor," Cole grumbled with mock anger.

"Not all the time." His hands were roaming over her bare shoulders and Lacey was shamelessly enjoying the sensations they were creating. "I left there some time past eleven."

He lifted his head, frowning, his gaze narrowing. "Where have you been since then?"

"I...I went for a walk on the beach."

'Alone?" Cole accused.

"Yes," she nodded, knowing it had been foolish.

"You deserve to be whipped within an inch of your life!" he stated gruffly. "You were actually walking on the beach for more than three hours?" He repeated her statement as if he still couldn't believe she had said it.

"I guess so, if that's how late it is." She couldn't bring herself to worry about the risk she had taken at this late date.

"Oh, Lacey...." He sighed heavily in exasperation

and crushed her tightly in his arms. "I knew I shouldn't have let you walk out of that door with Bowman."

"You couldn't have stopped me," she laughed softly. "I was so mad when I left that a brick wall couldn't have stopped me. And that's all your fault."

"My fault?" Cole tucked a finger under her chin, tilting her face up and gazing at it quizzically.

"You started the whole thing," she reminded him. "If you hadn't been so rude to Mike, I would never have lost my temper."

"What was I supposed to think?" An eyebrow twisted arrogantly at her answer. "I call his office and his secretary tells me he's out on a project. But when I get here, I find him carrying you around in his arms."

"You could have given him the benefit of the doubt," she pointed out, feeling the old resentment building again, "instead of jumping to conclusions that were completely wrong and unfair."

"How can you be so sure that my conclusion wasn't right?" Cole argued complacently.

"Because Mike isn't like that." Stiffening her arms against his chest, Lacey arched away from him. "He's honest and intelligent and works as hard as you do. Yours isn't the only project he's in charge of, and the delays on yours have been caused by suppliers and labor unions, things he has no control over."

Cole's mouth thinned grimly. "There you go again, defending him!"

"Well, what am I supposed to do when he isn't around to defend himself?" She twisted completely out of his arms.

When she would have walked away, he caught her

wrist, holding it firmly. "Lacey, I don't want to argue with you." His voice was husky, its demand low.

"No?" Looking into his dark blue eyes, Lacey knew that wasn't what he really wanted. "No, you want to make love, don't you?"

His gaze searched her face with unnerving thoroughness. "Don't you?" It was less a question than a request.

Lacey's pulse hammered in instant reaction, a heady intoxication filling her senses. She felt the pliant weakening of her flesh, but her mind refused to let its rule be overthrown by physical attraction.

"No." Her answer was faintly breathless, then firmer as she repeated it. "No, I don't."

"Liar," he accused, one corner of his mouth curving into an oddly bewitching smile.

Its charm was potent and Lacey had to breathe in deeply to keep it from weaving a spell around her. It took all of her willpower to remain impassive to his subtle and powerful appeal.

"You've accused me of that more than once, Cole," she said tightly. "And you're as wrong this time as you were all of the others."

With a quick tug, she pulled her wrist free of his hold and turned away. She could feel his gaze on her, compelling her back. She had to force herself to walk calmly and unhurriedly from him and not give in to the impulse to bolt to the safety of her room.

As she closed the bedroom door behind her, reaction set in, trembling through her with a violence that had her shaking. She was dangerously attracted to him. She recognized the symptoms, the combustible mixing of their two chemistries.

Cole was aware of it, too. He probably found her an attractive and highly available woman. His desire was part of the inherent danger of sharing the same house. Lacey knew she could never accept him as a temporary lover. It was neither wise nor sane.

A tear slipped from her lashes, its moistness surprising her as it trailed down her cheek. She flicked it away with her finger and began undressing for bed with jerky, harried movements.

One tear followed another. By the time she had her pajamas on and was crawling into bed, her cheeks were damp from the confusing sadness that made her heart ache.

As she was about to switch off the bedside light, her door was pushed open. Paralyzed, her fingers remained on the switch, unable to move. Cole stood in the doorway, his masculine bulk filling the frame. The roughly planed features of his face were set in implacable lines, cast half in shadow by the uneven light streaming over him. The rich umber shade of his hair gleamed nearly black. His eyes seemed afire with purpose and smoldering desire.

A wave of intense longing washed through Lacey and she rushed to deny it.

"Cole, I'm going to bed," she declared shakily.

"Yes," he agreed with a snap. His long strides carried him into the room, all the way to her bed. "But in my bed—where you belong!"

As he reached for her, Lacey made a strangled attempt to protest before realizing that words wouldn't stop him. She grabbed for the spare pillow on the double bed and threw it at him, hoping for a few seconds to escape his hands. But he knocked it aside with a swing of his arm and succeeded in grasping her waist before she could slide out the other side of the bed.

Effortlessly he slung her over his shoulder in a fireman's carry. Her bare feet flailed the air, finding no target. Her doubled fists, however, had a ready target and she pummeled at his broad shoulders and back, screaming abusively at his caveman tactics.

"Scream a little louder," Cole taunted insensitively. "No one can hear you, and you haven't broken my eardrums yet."

"You put me down!" Lacey choked.

The door to his bedroom was ajar and he kicked it the rest of the way open to carry her in and dump her unceremoniously on his bed. Her startled cry was muffled by the pillow onto which she fell. Stunned, it took her a second to react.

Rolling onto her side, she saw Cole shrugging out of his shirt. Along with it he seemed to be shedding the thin veneer of civilization that separated man from beast. Her stomach constricted at the sight of the naked expanse of chest, powerfully muscled yet sinuously lean.

As he reached to unbuckle his belt, she recovered from that momentary pang of desire and started to finish her roll off the bed. His hand snaked out to grip her shoulder and force her back.

The mattress sagged as it took his weight. Her struggles were to no avail as his superior strength pinned her shoulders to the bed. Half lying across her as he was, the crushing weight of his chest flattened her breasts. The body heat of his flesh burned through the thin silky material of her pajamas.

Her hands strained against the rippling muscles of his upper arms, futilely trying to push him away. By turning her head far to the side, she managed to elude his searching mouth, but that didn't stop it from exploring the area of her cheek and neck she had exposed. Despite her panicked attempts to get free, a response to his rough caresses shivered through her.

"Cole, what about the ground rules?" she gasped in alarm, her heart pounding frantically against her ribs.

"To hell with the ground rules," was his terse reply.

The warmth of his breath seemed to set fire to her skin, the flames quickly spreading, her flesh a ready tinderbox to be sparked by his touch. She didn't know how to douse the fire he was starting.

"You're tired, Cole. You don't know what you're doing," she protested weakly, not certain any longer if she knew what she was doing herself, or why.

"Maybe," he agreed in a throaty murmur that caressed her spine with its gruff, soft sound. "But I'm enjoying it, whatever it is."

His fingers slid beneath her cheek, curling into the short hair near her ear. He twisted her face toward him, his mouth at last finding the softness of her lips. Hungrily he explored their sweetness, devouring their token resistance until they were moving in response to his demands.

There was a roaring in her ears and Lacey realized it was the pounding of her heartbeat she heard. When her hands curled into his shoulders to cling to him, Cole shifted his attention, nuzzling her earlobe and chuckling softly in triumph.

"And you're enjoying it, too, little strawberry girl.

Don't deny it." Lightly he nipped her skin, the tiny pain becoming exquisite pleasure.

Her surrender wasn't complete and she began a protest, "Cole. . . ."

"Strawberry girl," he repeated, his moist mouth investigating the trembling curves of her lips. And the protest died in her throat. "Green and tart in the morning, ripely red and sweet at night."

Then his mouth was closing over hers again, his burning kiss drawing her into the vortex of his desire. Everything went spinning. Lacey felt like a wheel of fortune being spun around and around without knowing where or when she would stop, nor who would win or lose. It was a wild, dizzying merry-go-round.

His hands seemed to know exactly where to touch her and arouse her to the full pitch of sensual awareness. Boneless, she let her feminine curves be molded to fit his hard length.

Her hands slid over the steel-smooth skin of his back. She felt the pressure of his male need and the answering empty ache within her lower body.

At that instant she realized that she was losing control. She was letting herself be trapped in the whirlpool of his lust, the very thing she knew she didn't dare do.

"Don't do this, Cole, please," she whispered in aching protest, turning away from the drugging prowess of his kiss, a narcotic that was very addictive.

"Lacey, for God's sake," he muttered thickly, seeking her lips, "you know you want me to love you. I'll make you admit it."

Yes, she did want him to love her, but not just in the

physical sense. And his statement reaffirmed that belief. She continued her resistance.

"Do you always bully your women into submission?" She choked on the accusing demand.

Cole breathed in tightly, levering himself up on one elbow, the brilliant blue of his gaze glittering darkly over her profile. Lacey knew the advantage was hers and she couldn't weaken.

"Damn you, Lacey," he groaned finally, and rolled onto his back, dragging her with him.

His wide palm pressed her head against his bare chest, rising and falling in uneven breathing. Lacey could hear the hammering of his heart. Its beat was as erratic and aroused as her own.

She closed her eyes tightly, letting the circling steel band of his arms crush her to the comforting warmth of his chest.

He simply held her, making no further attempt to caress her or to carry out his threat to make her admit that she desired him as much as he wanted her. And she felt no fear in this embrace. The likelihood of seduction had suddenly faded.

But it was a long time before his pulse settled into a steady tempo and his breathing became relaxed and level. The contentment of lying in his arms was nearly as satisfying as his experienced lovemaking.

This warm glow and the late hour combined to make her eyelids heavy with sleep. Unwillingly she realized she had to leave the comfort of his arms, but as she started to disentangle herself from his hold, his muscles tightened, not letting her go.

"Stay here, Strawberry." His voice was husky with

sleep, a drowsily warm sound that she couldn't bring
herself to fight.

Cole, too, was minutes away from sleep. Lacey snug-
gled against his body heat, assuring herself that she
would stay just until he fell asleep, then she would leave.
At her lack of protest, he sighed, his breath stirring the
feathery shortness of her hair.

It wasn't easy staying awake. The one thing that
helped was the bedroom window that was propped
open. The cool breeze blowing in from the ocean and
moving the curtains danced over her skin, its brisk chill
just enough to keep her awake and aware of her surroundings.

At one particularly strong gust, Lacey shivered. Cole
immediately shifted her from his chest, reaching down
to pull the covers over both of them before nestling her
against his side again. The bed then became a warm co-
coon, relaxing and safe.

"Go to sleep, Strawberry," he whispered, and
brushed his mouth briefly across her hair. Despite the
casualness of the good-night caress, there was something intimately familiar about it.

"Yes," Lacey replied.

But of course she wouldn't really go to sleep. She was
only pretending to agree. When Cole was asleep she
would leave, she reminded herself.

Her lashes fluttered tiredly down and she decided to
rest her eyes just for a few minutes. His arm was a heavy
warm band around her waist, possessive and gentle.

# CHAPTER SEVEN

THE ALARM BUZZED loudly, almost right in Lacey's ear. She struggled to open her eyes, not understanding why it should be so loud.

A heavy weight was around her waist, pressing her to the mattress. She started to push it aside, irritated by the buzz and wishing Cole would shut his alarm clock off just once in the mornings.

As her fingers touched the weight, she felt the roughness of wiry hair and discovered the weight was an arm—Cole's arm, to be precise.

Instantly she was wide awake, remembering the events of last night—or more correctly, early morning. And the hard, long shape in the bed beside her was Cole.

Careful not to disturb him, she reached out, her fingertips just able to reach the alarm switch to turn off the noisy buzz. For once she was glad that Cole slept through his alarms. It would give her a chance to slip out of bed before he awakened.

But as she tried to slide away from him, he reached for her. "Don't move, Strawberry." His voice was thick with sleep.

Lacey guessed that it was a momentary alertness and within seconds he would again be sound asleep. "Your belt buckle is poking me," she lied, to explain the reason she had moved away from him.

Cole mumbled something unintelligible and rolled onto his side. Lacey remained completely still for several minutes until she was satisfied that he had fallen asleep. Then she slid silently out of bed and tiptoed to her own room.

Dressed and with coffee made and a glass of orange juice in her hand, she walked back to Cole's room. She paused in the doorway, gazing at the soundly sleeping figure. Sighing, she remembered how late it had been last night before Cole had slept, and the previous night when he had fallen asleep on the sofa. She simply couldn't bring herself to waken him and deprive him of the sleep he needed.

Turning around, she walked back to the kitchen and put the glass of juice in the refrigerator. The morning sunlight glistened on the ocean, reflecting its light into the living room.

With a cup of coffee in hand, Lacey moved onto the balcony. She hesitated, then descended the steps to the inviting stretch of empty beach. The silence of the morning was broken only by the waves licking the shore and the occasional cry of a seagull on the wing.

Only it wasn't quite empty, she discovered as she strolled along the sand. An older woman in a sunbonnet with jeans rolled up to her calves was wandering along, intent upon the treasures washed up by the tide.

Sitting down on the sand, Lacey watched the woman for a while before the soaring acrobatics of a seagull attracted her attention. The ocean was in one of its serene moods, its surface calm.

The peace surrounding Lacey caught her in its spell. She sat quietly on the sand, not conscious of thinking about anything, her mind seemingly blank.

Time seemed to slip away, the quarter hours seeming like seconds, so swiftly did they fly. Only the growing brightness of the rising sun and the increasing warmth of its rays offered any change. The ocean and sky remained the same and the woman was still scouring the beach for shells and driftwood.

"Lacey!" Cole impatiently shouted her name, breaking off the lonely cry of a gull.

Turning slightly on the sand to look over her shoulder, she saw him standing on the balcony, naked to the waist. Even at this distance, she could see how wrinkled his trousers were after their night of being slept in. His dark hair was tousled and he was attempting to comb it into order with his fingers.

She waved to him, her heart somersaulting in reaction to the blatant virility he possessed so early in the morning. It was impossible not to feel the attraction he radiated, primitively male and powerful.

"Why didn't you wake me?" he accused. "I was supposed to be at the office an hour ago."

"I thought you needed your sleep!" Lacey cupped her hands to her mouth to shout the answer.

"The next time, don't think. Wake me up!" His answering shout sounded more like a roar.

As he turned from the railing to enter the house, she stuck her tongue out at him, more amused than angered by his grouchy behavior.

Rising, she wandered toward the water. The woman combing the sand for seashells glanced up, and a smile wreathed her face, which was sun-lined despite the protective bonnet she wore.

"It's a beautiful morning, isn't it?" she commented.

"It certainly is," Lacey agreed, and paused near the woman. "Have you found very much this morning?"

"Nothing spectacular." The woman straightened from her bent position and pressed a hand to the small of her back.

"Do you collect shells?" Lacey glanced curiously at the pail slung over the woman's arm.

"Well, yes, I do," she admitted after a second's hesitation. "But my main hobby is making things with shells and other objects that I find on the beach."

"Like jewelry?" Lacey asked, noticing the string of shell beads around the woman's neck.

The woman touched the necklace with her finger. "Yes, jewelry—mostly earrings and necklaces. At the moment I'm making a picture with shells. That's why I'm collecting all of these little mauve shells," she explained, reaching into the bucket to lift out a handful of the tiny shells. "There are any number of things you can make with shells—mobiles, wind chimes, lots of things."

"Sounds fascinating," murmured Lacey with a trace of envy in her voice. Her creative talents seldom stretched to more than attempting a floral arrangement from time to time.

"It's very enjoyable," the woman stated. "And now that I've retired, it keeps me busy."

"Lacey!" Cole was calling to her again and she turned to the house in answer. He stood on the balcony, this time dressed in a tan leisure suit. "I'm leaving now. I'll see you tonight."

Lacey waved her understanding of his shouted message. After a brief salute, he walked into the house. She smiled faintly to herself, amused by the difference a morning cup of coffee and a shower could make to his disposition.

"That was thoughtful of your husband," the woman commented. "My John always lets me know when he's leaving the house, too."

"Cole isn't my husband." Lacey made the correction automatically and without thinking.

"Oh." The woman was momentarily startled by the answer. "Oh!" The second time, the word was drawn out with dawning understanding and a widened look of shock and vague disapproval at her conclusion.

Lacey went scarlet, realizing that the implication of her statement was that she and Cole were living together although unmarried. Correcting the impression would involve a long, detailed explanation of the circumstances surrounding their decision to share the house. But Lacey didn't attempt to justify their arrangement. She wasn't certain the woman would believe her anyway.

"I have some cleaning to do at the house. Have a nice day." Lacey offered, and self-consciously made her exit from the beach.

As she walked away, she heard the woman murmuring to herself, "These young people nowadays—they seem to have lost all sense of moral values!"

Lacey compressed her lips into a thin line and kept walking.

In actual fact, there was very little to do at the house, but she puttered around doing odds and ends, watering the plants, taking care of some hand washing until after noon. With a sandwich and some fruit, she lunched on the balcony, then settled into one of the lounge chairs with a book.

The sun was warm and relaxing. Its effect combined with the lack of regular sleep over the last two nights made her drowsy, and soon she was setting her book aside to take a short nap.

The next time she opened her eyes, they focused on the familiar brown leather briefcase. Immediately she looked for its owner and found Cole sitting in one of the deck chairs, his long legs stretched out in front of him and a can of beer in his hand. Dark spiky lashes screened the expression in his eyes, but he was watching her.

His mouth twitched briefly in a smile. "So you're finally going to wake up, sleepyhead. I thought for a while that you were going to sleep around the clock."

Stifling a yawn with the back of her hand, Lacey pushed herself up on an elbow, ignoring his teasing comment to ask, "What time is it?"

"Four-thirty or thereabouts." He shrugged, uninterested in the exact time although his gold watch was around his wrist, making it easily verified.

"I didn't realize I was so tired." She rubbed her eyes and covered another yawn with her hand. "How long have you been here?"

"Since shortly after two."

Which was only a little while after she had fallen asleep. "You haven't been sitting there all that time?" She blinked in disbelief.

Cole nodded. "Watching you sleep."

The grogginess was leaving rapidly and she was becoming more alert with each passing second. And she noticed the faint suggestion of weariness in his posture.

"You should have napped, too, instead of watching me," she said, sitting upright.

"Maybe," he conceded, "but I wanted to be here when you woke up."

It seemed a curious reason. "Why?"

"Because I wanted to apologize for last night."

"Oh." His statement suddenly made her uneasy, especially with that dark blue gaze watching her so intently through the narrowed slit of his lashes.

She walked to the balcony railing, wishing Cole had pretended last night had never happened rather than alluding to it on their first real meeting. At the same instant, she realized that she had escaped to the beach in the morning before he had awakened to avoid this confrontation after the events of last night.

Footsteps indicated his approach and she tensed herself, her heart beating as rapidly as a hummingbird's wings. Cole stopped directly behind her and she could feel the disturbing touch of his gaze.

"Aren't you going to accept my apology?" he questioned.

"For what?" She shrugged nervously. "Nothing happened."

"Not for lack of intention," he said in a gently mocking voice.

Lacey was flustered. All her poise was gone and she felt as skittish as a schoolgirl. What had happened to all her maturity, her confidence to handle any kind of a situation? What power did Cole have to reduce her to a quivering mass of nerves?

His hands curled lightly on her shoulders to turn her around. She stared at his shirt collar, the top two buttons unfastened, giving her a glimpse of his bare chest. It was just about as unnerving as gazing into his magnetic blue eyes.

He crooked a finger under her chin to lift her head. "I knew you'd be a temptation from the first night when we made our agreement, but I thought I could handle it." He paused, frowning at the agitation darkening her brown eyes. "I was tired and irritable last night. And we'd argued over Bowman—"

"Cole, please," Lacey interrupted tightly, "I don't want to dissect all the events and emotions that led up to last night. Exposing them to daylight doesn't change anything. Don't do this to me."

"Don't do this to you?" He laughed without humor. "What about what you do to me?"

Seemingly of their own volition, his hands began lightly rubbing her shoulders and upper arms in what amounted to a circular caress, with Cole completely unconscious of what he was doing. It produced a bone-melting sensation and Lacey knew just how dangerous that was. But she seemed powerless to stop it.

"Do you know how I felt when you drove so recklessly away from here yesterday?" His voice lowered to an intimately husky pitch, vaguely fierce and demanding. "Or when I found out that you weren't with Bowman? Do you know what it was like waiting for you to come home last night?" His fingers dug briefly into her flesh. "Do you know what it's like going to bed each night and imagining you in the next room in your cute little pajamas?''

She knew she was a breath away from surrendering to his attraction. ''Then leave. Move out,'' she challenged in desperation rather than let her senses lead her down the garden path of temptation.

''And worry about you being here by yourself at the mercy of vandals and burglars?'' Cole argued. ''That would be going from the frying pan to the fire. I'd be trading cold showers for ulcers.''

''I suppose you want me to move out, then,'' she said stiffly.

''It would solve things.''

''Would it?'' she countered with a funny ache in her throat.

''I don't know....'' Cole sighed heavily, releasing her to turn away. Raking his fingers roughly through his hair, he let his hand rest on the back of his head, rubbing the tight cords in his neck.

''Good, because I'm not moving out,'' she declared, even though every ounce of logic in her mind cried out that's what she should do. ''If you'll excuse me—'' she started for the door to the house ''—I'll see what there is for dinner tonight.''

''No!'' Cole spur around, the savage bite in his voice stopping her. ''We'll eat out tonight.''

She hesitated for only a split second. ''You can eat out if you want. I'll fix something here for myself.''

She had refused his invitation, finding the prospect of going out with him on what would seem like a date as unsettling as staying in the house alone with him for the evening.

"Dammit, Lacey," he muttered, "I thought I'd made myself clear. I'm not letting you stay in this house alone at night. It's bad enough that you're by yourself in the daytime."

"You're not letting me!" Lacey flared at his arrogant statement.

"That's right, I'm not letting you," he repeated forcefully. "And you can argue about that for as long as you like, but either we both go or we both stay. That is the way it's going to be. If you're sensible, you'll agree to go out to dinner with me so we can get out of this house and be among some people."

Their eyes locked in a clashing, silent duel that lasted for several explosive seconds before Cole challenged, "Which is it going to be?"

There wasn't really any choice. "Give me a few minutes to change clothes," Lacey agreed grudgingly.

"Fine." The roughness hadn't completely left his tone. "We'll go somewhere for a before-dinner cocktail first," he told her.

It was only after they had left the cocktail lounge for the restaurant that the tension between them began to ease. They were seated by the hostess at a table with a view of the ocean, outside spotlights directed at the rolling whitecaps of the surf.

"What looks good to you?" Cole asked, glancing up from his menu to Lacey.

"I'm trying to decide whether to have the deviled crab or the steamed blue crab," she answered, nibbling thoughtfully at her lower lip.

"Have both," he offered as an alternative.

"Are you kidding? I'd be so full I couldn't move.

You'd have to carry me out of here," she joked, dismissing his suggestion.

"It wouldn't be the first time I've carried you somewhere," he reminded her quietly.

The way he was looking at her made her glow warm all over. She immediately stared at her menu, aware of his soft, almost silent chuckle. She closed the menu and set it on the table in front of her.

"I'll have the steamed crab," she decided quickly in an effort to divert the subject.

The waiter appeared at Cole's left. "The steamed blue crab for each of us," he ordered. "And a wine list, please."

When the waiter left, a silence ensued. Lacey nervously fingered the prongs of her fork, unable to think of any small talk, which had carried the first part of the evening. Cole reached out, covering her hand completely with his own to still its nervous fidgeting.

"I was only teasing you," he offered in apology, "when I reminded you about last night."

"I know, but it's nothing to joke about."

She glanced up and found she was unable to look away from his compelling gaze. Her heart turned over, its crazy flip-flop not helping the tingling warmth shooting up her arm from his hand.

"Well, well, well," a male voice declared mockingly from behind Lacey. "You two have finally ventured out of your little love nest!"

As Lacey tried to pull her hand free of Cole's, his fingers tightened around it, refusing to let her go. His gaze flicked to the voice.

"Hello, Vic." A bland mask slipped into place to conceal his expression.

At that moment the handsome blond-haired man stepped into Lacey's view. Cole's use of the man's name had already jogged her memory into placing the voice as that of Monica's brother.

"Hello, Cole." He nodded first to him, then turned his cynically distant smile to Lacey. "We meet again, Lacey Andrews."

"Hello, Mr. Hamilton." She returned his greeting with deliberate formality, not liking his spoiled, arrogant attitude any more now than she had at their first meeting.

"Vic," he corrected, and widened his smile, which didn't make it any warmer or more charming. "My sister has been gnashing her teeth over you all week. Really, Cole—" he turned his attention away from Lacey "—I think you could have let her down a little more gently."

"I've been letting her down gently for two years," Cole replied dryly. "It's time she realized it."

"I think she's become convinced that you'll be the master in any marriage," Vic commented absently. "Monica always has been very liberal, willing to forgive you for your little diversions—your pillow friends." He glanced pointedly at Lacey, who was bristling half in anger and half in embarrassment.

Cole's mouth twisted wryly. "Is that what Monica said?"

"She did suggest that I might pass the message on if I happened to run into you," Vic admitted smoothly.

"You've delivered it," Cole stated with apparent indifference.

"Now you want me to run along and leave you alone, is that it?" Vic shrugged. "Very well. Enjoy your evening."

When he had retreated out of hearing, Lacey sputtered indignantly, "Why didn't you correct him? He isn't Monica."

An eyebrow was arched mockingly. "Correct him about your being my 'pillow friend?' Would you have me deny that we've slept together?"

"You know it was perfectly innocent," she retorted.

Releasing her hand, he leaned back in his chair, studying her thoughtfully and just a little bit coolly. "You're very anxious to deny any relationship between us whenever Vic has been around. Are you attracted to him?"

"Of course not!" Lacey denied the allegation vigorously.

"The Hamiltons are very wealthy, and by some people's standards, Vic could be classified as a very handsome man. He'd be quite a catch in matrimonial circles."

"I'm sure the same could be said for Monica, couldn't it?" she argued.

"It could," he agreed. "But we aren't talking about Monica."

"I'm not talking about Vic, but maybe you should take his advice and get Monica's forgiveness. Then the two of you can get back together."

His mouth thinned. "You do enjoy starting arguments, don't you, Lacey?"

"I don't start them. You do."

"Let's end this one by dropping the subject," he suggested briskly.

"Gladly," Lacey agreed.

The waiter arrived with their dinner, negating the need for immediate conversation to fill the awkward silence. With good food and a glass of New York wine, the silence was soon reduced to a companionable level.

"How is the project coming?" Lacey inquired, using her knife to pry off the apron flap on the underside of the crab.

"Very well. Didn't Bowman mention that the men were making up for lost time?" Cole asked idly.

"No." With the top shell discarded, Lacey broke off the toothed claws and set them aside to free the meat from them later. "He didn't mention it at all."

"Considering the lost time that's been made up, I would have thought he would have been bragging about it." There was nothing derogatory in his comment.

"Mike doesn't brag about his work," Lacey stated. "He considers it his duty to do the best that he can. He never lets a problem become an excuse. He tries to solve it, which is why it was so unfair when you blamed him for the delays on your project."

Cole ignored the last red flag remark. "Bowman mentioned the two of you had been discussing business, so I presumed he was referring to the progress on the project. What were you talking about, or am I treading on forbidden ground with that question?" Amusement glittered faintly in the look he gave her.

Lacey hesitated, her knife poised to slice lengthwise through the center of the crab, now broken in half. "When did you ask Mike what we had been discussing?"

"When you were in your room, changing clothes to leave with him."

"And he told you we were talking about business?"

"Yes. At the time I found it very difficult to believe. There aren't many men I know, who can hold an attractive woman in their arms and talk business," Cole admitted.

"And you still find it difficult to believe, don't you?" she challenged.

"With you, I'm learning that anything is possible." The laugh lines around his eyes deepened, but his mouth didn't smile. "Were you talking business?"

"We were talking about the girl who's replaced me while I'm on vacation," she explained. "Mechanically Donna is an excellent secretary, but her personality can be very irritating."

"I've talked to her a couple of times." Cole nodded without elaborating any further.

"Then you understand what Mike has been going through this last week?" A smile teased the corners of her mouth.

"And sympathize," he added dryly. "But that doesn't explain why he was dangling you over the railing."

"Oh, that." Lacey didn't attempt to hide her smile this time. "I was teasing him. I told him I was considering handing in my notice and suggesting Donna as my replacement. He was threatening murder if I did."

"Are you thinking of quitting?"

She dug out a forkful of the exposed crab meat, shaking her head. "No, I like my job."

"What about when you get married? Will you still work?" Cole was slicing his crab, not even glancing up as he asked the question.

It was difficult to make a casual response. If anyone else had asked, she could have laughed away the question, but she was more than half in love with Cole right now. Marriage became a subject that sent quivers down her spine.

"More than likely I'd have to keep working after I married to make ends meet," she answered, self-consciously avoiding looking at Cole when she spoke.

"Would you mind?"

"No. As I said, I like my job and I don't think a lot of idle time would suit me. I like to be doing constructive and challenging things." That she could answer truthfully and without hesitation.

"What if your husband didn't want you to work? What if he wanted you at home?" Cole lifted his wine glass, flicking a glance at her over the rim.

"We'd probably have an argument. Are you one of those old-fashioned men who don't approve of working wives?" Lacey asked, suddenly curious.

"I don't mind if it's other men's wives that are working, but I'm not certain how I would react if it were my own wife." Cole smiled, and it had a devastating effect on Lacey's senses. "When we have children, I suppose I would insist she be home with them, at least when they're small."

"When the children are little, I would want to be home with them," Lacey agreed readily.

"Do you mean we've found something else we can agree on besides sharing the same house?" Cole declared with mock astonishment, a wicked glint in his indigo blue eyes. "Remarkable," he drawled, and Lacey laughed.

Their earlier disagreement over Vic and Monica Hamilton was forgotten. They seemed to find a surfeit of things to talk about without becoming embroiled in any controversy.

All too soon, it seemed, Cole was driving the car into the garage. In truth, they had lingered over dessert, then coffee, until it was nearly ten.

Concealing a sigh of regret that the evening was coming to a close, Lacey stepped out of the car, instinctively taking the door key from her purse. Both stepped forward at the same time to unlock the connecting door, bumping into each other.

"Allow me," Cole offered with a mocking inclination of his head.

"By all means," she agreed, replacing the key in her purse.

In the lower entrance hall he paused to lock the door behind him while she slowly began to climb the steps. She was reluctant to have the evening end so soon.

"Shall I—" she began.

"Let's make a pact," Cole interrupted, a step behind her on the stairs. "You don't offer to make coffee or a nightcap and I won't suggest showing you my etchings."

"All right," Lacey agreed without enthusiasm.

She knew exactly why he had said that. They were back in the house again, and its privacy and isolation invited an intimacy they were both trying to avoid.

His hand lightly took hold of her elbow, his touch disquietingly impersonal, and guided her across the living room to the hall leading to the bedrooms. As they started down the hall, Lacey wanted to protest that she wasn't sleepy, but she knew it wasn't wise and kept silent.

At the closed door of her bedroom they stopped, and Lacey turned hesitantly toward him. An elemental tension crackled between them.

"Do you know this is the first time I've escorted a girl directly to her bedroom door to say good night?" Cole joked wryly.

"It's a first for me, too." Lacey tried to respond in the same vein, but her voice sounded husky and as unnerved by his nearness as she felt.

His large palm cupped the side of her face in a caress that was gentle rather than arousing. "You'd better go straight to bed," he said. "After these last couple of days, you need a good night's sleep."

Something in the way he said it made her ask, "What about you? Aren't you going to bed right away?"

"No." There was a short negative shake of his head. "I thought I'd take a walk along the beach before turning in."

"But I—" Lacey started to suggest that she might go along, but his thumb pressed her lips into silence.

"No," he refused abruptly, his gaze sliding to her mouth. "I know what I'm doing, Lacey."

Her heart was skipping beats all over the place and her brown eyes were round and luminous. She nodded briefly her agreement and anger sparkled darkly in his eyes.

"Don't be so damned meek," Cole growled. "It doesn't suit you."

"I—" Lacey started to defend her action.

"Just shut up," he interrupted, and she detected the

faint groan in his throat before he let his mouth replace the thumb that had been pressed against her lips.

The hard, searing kiss flamed through her as his arms crushed her against his male length. The lean warmth of his body added to the fire already raging inside her. The fierce, sensual masculinity about him, almost tangible, was irresistible to her feminine core.

Her lips parted under the bruising urgency of his mouth, permitting him to deepen the kiss with shattering expertise. She felt his tenseness, his muscles like coiled springs in an effort to keep control, while she herself had none. But she had long ago realized that in Cole's arms she lost her inhibition, and that made his touch doubly dangerous.

Abruptly he broke off the kiss, lifting his head. A muscle twitched convulsively along his powerful jaw as he stared grimly into her dazed, love-softened face. He breathed in deeply and pivoted away.

"Good night, Lacey," he ordered.

For an instant she was incapable of speech. "Good night," she answered finally, but he was already striding into the living room, not glancing back when she spoke.

Not until she heard the sliding door to the balcony open and close did she enter her bedroom. She was emotionally shaken by the feelings and sensations he had aroused. She knew she couldn't sleep so she walked to the window, gazing out at the moon casting a pale silvery light on the sand.

In seconds Cole was in her view, long strides carrying him toward the waves. His hands were thrust deep in his pockets and his attention fixed on the ground. Lacey watched him until he walked out of her sight, striding along the beach into the night.

Changing into her pajamas, she crawled into bed. She didn't attempt to close her eyes as she listened to the clock on the bedside table tick the seconds away. The hands of the clock were nearly clasped together to signal the midnight hour when she finally heard Cole enter the house.

His pace had slowed considerably as he wandered into the hallway. He stopped outside her door. When she saw the doorknob turn, she closed her eyes, feigning sleep.

Opening the door, Cole made no attempt to enter the room, but stared at her for several silent minutes before he closed the door. She heard him walk to his own room. The pounding of her heart became almost an aching pain as she turned onto her side and tried to sleep.

# CHAPTER EIGHT

THE NEXT MORNING Lacey awoke early from habit. She lay in bed for several minutes listening to the sounds of Cole stirring about.

Finally she climbed out of bed, realizing that she couldn't get back to sleep and that she would have to get up sooner or later. Pulling on her housecoat, she walked into the hall.

At that moment Cole stepped out of his room softly whistling a tuneless melody. He was wearing swimming trunks, chocolate brown with tan stripes. He smiled when he saw her.

"Good morning," he greeted her cheerfully.

"You must have been up for a while," Lacey observed, her own voice still husky from sleep.

"I have. How did you know? Did I wake you?" he questioned, waiting for her and falling into step beside her.

"No, you didn't. I just guessed you'd been up because you're usually grouchy when you first wake up," she replied.

He reached out and ruffled her short hair. "You aren't exactly Miss Sunshine when you first get up in the mornings, either," he commented.

"Don't do that!" she protested, and tried to brush her hair down with the flat of her hand.

"See what I mean?" He winked, an impish light dancing in his dark blue eyes.

"I never have claimed to be Miss Sunshine," she pointed out. "Did you make coffee?"

"Not yet. I was on my way out for a morning swim before breakfast, hoping you'd be up and have it ready when I came in," he replied with engaging honesty, the mocking amusement still gleaming in his look.

"You could have fixed it and had it ready for me when I got up," she countered, unable to take offense this early in the day.

"I could have," he agreed. "Would you like to come for a swim with me? I'll wait."

"No, thanks," Lacey refused, not glancing at his lean, browned physique, which was altogether too disturbingly virile for her senses to cope with when she wasn't fully awake yet.

"Okay," he shrugged, branching away from her toward the balcony door. "I'll see you later."

He seemed to take much of the morning sunshine with him when he left. Lacey halfheartedly fixed the coffee pot and plugged it in. She took her orange juice onto the balcony, her gaze searching the waves until she found Cole. He was a strong swimmer, as she had guessed he would be. She watched him for a long time before finally reminding herself to get dressed.

Showering first, she put on shorts of tan plaid with a white boat-necked top. The coffee was perked when she returned to the kitchen. She poured a cup and wandered again to the balcony, her gaze once more drawn magnetically to the beach.

Two figures caught her attention. One was Cole

wading out of the ocean, lifting a hand in greeting to the second figure. It was the woman in the sunbonnet to whom Lacey had talked the previous morning.

She paled slightly as Cole stopped to talk to the woman searching the beach for shells. His tanned body glistened like bronze from the moistness of the water beading over his skin.

Lacey had no idea what the two were talking about, but Cole was listening with obvious attention. Once he glanced to the house, spying Lacey on the balcony.

Apprehension shivered over her skin. The woman surely wouldn't mention her impression that she and Cole were living together. Surely she wouldn't be that bold?

Soon Cole was nodding a goodbye to the woman, his long legs striding across the sands to the balcony stairs. Lacey was tempted to retreat into the house, but she forced herself to stand her ground and react calmly to his return.

"Did you have a good swim?" she asked.

"Great." His hair glistened darkly in the sunlight as he effortlessly took the steps two at a time to reach the top. "Ah, the coffee's done," he said, seeing the cup in Lacey's hand.

"I'll get you a cup," she offered quickly, finding an excuse to leave.

"It can wait." He walked to the railing near her, leaning both hands on it and gazing silently at the ocean beyond.

Then, unexpectedly, he looked at her, his gaze piercing yet with a roguish glint in it. He was so vibrant and male, a bronzed statue come to life, that her breath was coming in uneven spurts.

"I just had a very intriguing conversation with that woman on the beach," he said. "A Mrs. Carlyle—she lives a few houses down. Do you know her?"

Something in the inflection of his voice told Lacey that he already knew the answer, possibly recognizing the woman from yesterday.

"I talked to her for a few minutes the other day," she admitted, "but I didn't know her name." Slightly flustered, she knew there was a tinge of pink in her cheeks. She sipped quickly at her coffee, pretending the tepid liquid was hot. "She collects shells and makes things with them, jewelry and such."

"So she told me—among other things." There was a hint of laughter in his reply, but his mockingly intent gaze did not relent an inch. "I'm curious about what you told her."

"Me?" Lacey swallowed nervously.

"You're aware that Mrs. Carlyle is under the impression that we're living together in the immoral interpretation of the phrase?" he murmured.

"I was afraid she thought that," Lacey admitted after a second's hesitation.

"What did you tell her?" he prodded, a smile playing with the corners of his mouth.

"She assumed we were married and I automatically said you weren't my husband. She drew her own conclusions from that," she explained self-consciously.

"And you didn't correct her assumption?"

"It would have been such a long drawn-out story, and she was a stranger." She shrugged and curled both hands around her coffee cup. "What did she say to you?"

"I was on the receiving end of a very stern lecture." The creases deepened on either side of his mouth, his amusement at Lacey's obvious discomfort.

"Oh," was all she could think to say, and she stared at her half-empty cup of coffee.

Cole reached out and removed the cup from her hands, setting it on a deck table. Before she could protest that action, he was curving both arms around her. She pressed her hands against his chest, her fingers coming in contact with the cloud of moist dark hairs.

"She was trying to convince me that if I had any respect for you at all, I'd make an honest woman out of you." He smiled down at her, the dampness of his legs against her thighs evoking a roughly warm sensation. "And I haven't even found out how dishonest you can be."

"Cole, please!" Her throat had constricted and she had to force the words out.

He bent his head to brush his mouth over the soft curve of her jaw. The tangy ocean scent clinging to his skin assailed her senses, already turned upside down by his touch. He teased the sensitive skin of her neck, his breath dancing warm over her flesh.

"Shall I make an honest woman out of you, Lacey?" he mused playfully, not a serious note in his voice.

She quickly swallowed to ease the tightness in her throat and pushed away from his disturbing nearness. "Don't be ridiculous, Cole!" She couldn't joke about a thing like marriage.

He made no attempt to recapture her as he watched

her widen the distance between them with quick, retreating steps. Yet behind the glitter of teasing amusement, his expression seemed to be curiously guarded and alert.

"Maybe I should make a dishonest woman of you first," he said again in that same laughing tone, to indicate he was teasing.

Lacey felt light-headed and quite unable to match his bantering words. "Maybe you should have some coffee to sober you up. You've had either too much ocean or too much sun," she suggested.

"I don't want coffee now." The inflection of his answer implied he wanted something else.

The undercurrents vibrating in the air seemed to increase in voltage. Lacey paled, unsure how much more of this electrically charged atmosphere she could tolerate before succumbing to its force. She nearly jumped out of her skin when Cole moved unexpectedly.

But he swept past her, speaking abruptly. "I'll shower and dress first, then have coffee."

"I'll start breakfast," she offered, in need of something to say. She was trembling uncontrollably from the aftershocks, but Cole wasn't there to see her reaction.

Bacon was sizzling in the skillet when he entered the kitchen, wearing khaki trousers and a short-sleeved pullover top of white knit. The clinging fabric accented the width of his shoulders and molded the muscled leanness of his torso. The clean fragrance of soap mingled with the musky scent of his after-shave lotion.

Lacey couldn't help being aware of the heady combination as he helped himself to the coffee and moved to the counter near the stove. He was brimming with vitality, positively overpowering her with the force of his presence. She began turning the bacon strips to keep them from burning, aware that he was watching her intently with his disconcerting gaze.

"Do you have to stare at me like that?" she asked impatiently, not letting her own gaze wander from the frying bacon in the skillet. "It makes me feel as if I've suddenly grown two heads."

"Sorry." Offhandedly Cole made the apology and sipped at his coffee. "Do you have any plans for today?"

"Plans?" she echoed.

"Yes." A brow twisted in amusement at the darting blank look she gave him. "Are you expecting Bowman or anyone over for the day?"

"No, he didn't mention he'd be stopping by," she qualified, and added a glob of butter to the egg skillet, turning on the fire beneath it.

The bacon grease popped, splattering the back of her hand, and she jumped back from the stove with a muffled exclamation of pain. Cole immediately had a hold of her arm, practically dragging her to the sink. Turning on the cold water tap, he thrust her hand beneath the running water.

"Keep it there," he ordered.

"The bacon will burn," protested Lacey.

"I'll watch it. You just let that cold water run on that burn for a while," he ordered, moving back to the stove to rescue the bacon. Lacey did as she was told, and the stinging pain was gradually reduced to a numbness.

"How does it feel?" he asked when she turned off the water to dry her hand.

"It's fine." There was a barely discernible red mark where the hot grease had splattered on her hand.

"Aren't you going to ask me why I was wondering if you'd made any plans for today?" He broke an egg into the melted butter in the second skillet.

She hesitated. "Why?"

"I thought if you hadn't made any other arrangements, we'd drive over to the Eastern Shore for the day." He added another egg to the skillet. "How would you like your eggs cooked?"

"Over easy." Lacey answered his last question first; it was the easiest.

"What about going over to the Eastern Shore?"

"It sounds like a good idea," she agreed.

"Good," he nodded. "Have you put the bread in the toaster yet?"

"Not yet." And Lacey reached for the bread.

AN HOUR LATER their breakfast was over and the dishes washed, and they were on their way to the Eastern Shore of Virginia. Traversing the seventeen-mile-long Chesapeake Bay bridge-tunnel, Lacey watched a navy ship some distance away in the Atlantic Ocean to her right. Its silhouette moved steadily closer to the ship channel leading to the waters of Chesapeake Bay on her left.

But Lacey didn't look to her left at the warships and merchant vessels more easily viewed in the waters of the bay. The confines of the car had heightened her awareness of Cole, if that was possible.

Without glancing at him, she was conscious of everything about him, from the way his dark brown hair curled near his shirt collar to the strength of his sunbrowned hands on the wheel. An inbred radar system seemed tuned strictly to his presence.

"Any place special you want to see when we get over there?" he asked, his gaze sliding from the road to her for a brief instant.

"No." Lacey shook her head, unable to think of a single place she particularly wanted to visit.

"Let's drive to Chincoteague," he suggested.

They were approaching the concrete island in the bay where the bridge dipped beneath the water to become the tunnel under the ship channel.

"That's nearly a hundred miles, isn't it?" She frowned, turning to study his strongly defined profile.

"About that," he agreed blandly. The cavernous tunnel swallowed them, a ribbon of lights overhead.

She glanced at her watch. "Do you realize how late it will be when we get back? You have to work tomorrow. You should have an early night."

There was a wry, upward curve of his mouth, but his gaze never left the tunnel stretching ahead of them. "Let's avoid the subject of sleep and beds, Lacey, and enjoy the day," he suggested.

Jerking her head to the front, she stared straight ahead at the sunlight beckoning at the tunnel exit. A spurt of anger flashed through her at his unnecessary comment.

His hand reached out to clasp the back of her neck. His fingers felt the taut muscles and began to massage them gently.

"Relax, Lacey," he ordered in a coaxing tone. "And stop hugging the car door. I'm not going to bite."

"Aren't you?" she retorted, already stung by the point of Cupid's arrow.

"I promise." He smiled. "No bites—not even an occasional nibble!"

With that his gaze slid to the exposed curve of her throat, its brushing touch as effective as a caress. Immediately he withdrew his hand and returned it to the steering wheel.

"This afternoon we're just going to be a couple taking a Sunday drive," he stated.

And Lacey felt a twinge of regret that it was to be so, regardless of how sensible it was. But it was only because he was so attractive. She managed a stiff smile of agreement to his suggestion.

The Cape Charles lighthouse poked its silhouette into the skyline, signaling that land was near. Shortly the bridge curved to an end on the jutting finger of land that was Virginia's Eastern Shore.

The modern highway carved its way up the length of the unspoiled peninsula. Lacey caught glimpses of the windswept Atlantic coast and the islands scattered out from its beaches.

It was impossible to remain immune to the charm of the landscape for long. Its beauty was tireless, entrapping her in its spell, the minutes slipping by as fast as the miles.

As they neared the Maryland border, Cole turned off the main highway, crossing the bridge to the island of Chincoteague. They traveled through the small town of the same name and on across a second bridge to Assateague Island.

Declared a national seashore, the island was the refuge for the wild Chincoteague ponies, believed to be descendants of horses from the wreck of a Spanish galleon more than four hundred years ago. On the island they ran free as their ancestors did, drinking from the freshwater pools and grazing in the nutritious salt marshes. Inbreeding over the years had stunted the horses to pony size, yet the clean-limbed, delicate conformation remained in the descendants.

To keep the herds' numbers at a level the island food supply could support, there was a roundup every year by the residents of neighboring Chincoteague Island. The sick and injured among the ponies were treated and a certain number of the new crop of foals was sold at auction.

Although there was a bridge to connect the Assateague Island refuge with Chincoteague Island, tradition demanded that the ponies swim the short distance between the two islands. The annual July event drew thousands of visitors to witness it and attend the auction.

There was no one around, though, when Cole and Lacey spied a herd of the small ponies and stopped to watch them. The pinto stallion kept a wary eye on them and they took care not to alarm him. He tolerated their presence at that distance, leaving Lacey and Cole free to watch the antics of a cavorting pair of young foals.

The approach of a second party was more than the stallion would permit to invade his domain. With his head snaking low to the ground, he began moving his mares away, nipping at the recalcitrant ones slow to obey his commands.

"They're beautiful!" Lacey breathed when the last of the ponies trotted out of sight ahead of the stallion.

"Are you glad you came?" Cole asked, smiling.

"Of course," she responded naturally, the bemused light still in her brown eyes.

"So am I," he agreed, and glanced at his watch. "We aren't likely to see any more this afternoon. I don't know about your stomach, but mine says it's been a long time since breakfast. Let's go back to Chincoteague and find a place to have dinner before starting back."

The summer sun was setting as they finally began the trek back to Virginia Beach. Its golden glow gave a serene ending to a relaxing afternoon and evening. Somewhere along the long ride, Lacey closed her eyes and forgot to open them. The next thing she was aware of was a hand gently nudging her awake.

"We're home, Strawberry," Cole's low voice came to her through the drugging mists of sleep.

Lazily raising her lashes, she focused on his bent figure, holding the car door open. She smiled at him, unaware of the curious dreamlike quality to her expression.

"Already?" she murmured.

"Yes, already," he answered dryly, his helping hand more or less forcing her out of the car.

Not fully awake, she took advantage of the support he offered, leaning heavily on him as they walked slowly to the garage entrance to the house. His arm remained around the back of her waist until they reached the top of the stairs and the living room.

"I think I'd better put some coffee on," Lacey murmured, trying to blink the sandman's dust from her eyes.

"No need to bother to make it for me." Cole moved away from her to the sofa, bending down to pick up his briefcase.

She watched him sit down and open the briefcase on his lap. "What are you doing?" she asked, frowning.

"I have some work to do," he answered without looking up.

"After all that driving?" She couldn't believe he was serious.

"It has to be done," he replied, taking out a folder and his note pad.

Within seconds, Lacey was completely shut out. She stood uncertainly in the center of the room before finally wandering out onto the balcony.

Leaning against the railing, she experienced a curiously letdown feeling. The night sky was alight with stars that seemed to stretch on as endlessly as the emptiness inside of her.

Shivering, she reentered the house. "It's getting chilly out," she commented, but the temperature inside seemed several degrees cooler after Cole's indifferent nod. "Do you have to work?" she demanded in a flash of irritation.

There was a remoteness in the blue gaze that sliced to her. "I don't happen to be on vacation, Lacey," he reminded her.

"I wish I weren't," she declared, suddenly regretting the moment she had met him.

He turned back to his papers muttering, "So do I. Then you wouldn't be here. You'd be in your own apartment where you belong."

"That's what you want, isn't it? For me to move out?" she challenged tightly, a pain squeezing her chest like a constricting band.

Again his cool, glittering blue eyes regarded her with

a level look. "I thought I'd made it plain that was what I've wanted all along."

Lacey paled slightly. "I had the impression you'd changed your mind," she retorted.

There was an unfriendly gleam of mockery in his gaze. "Because I had a desire to make love to you?" he replied. "For God's sake, Lacey, you're an attractive woman, intelligent and easy to be with, as well as having a passionate nature. Any man in my situation would want to make love to you, given the opportunity."

"I see," Lacey murmured stiffly.

If she had asked him outright whether or not he felt any serious affection toward her, she couldn't have received a more explicit answer. The passes he had made at her had been strictly that—just passes.

She was available and had been available. She should have been glad that he wasn't the unscrupulous type that would have taken advantage of her vulnerability. But the ache inside was too painful to leave room for gratitude for small favors.

"Now, if you'll excuse me, I'll get back to work." Cole shuffled his papers, bending over them again. She was being dismissed.

"By all means, go ahead," Lacey urged on a spiteful note of sarcasm. "Don't let me disturb you whatever you do," she added.

"You disturb me just by being here," he muttered almost beneath his breath, but he did not let his gaze wander from the papers in his hand.

She had the impression that he hadn't meant her to hear the remark, but there was no consolation in that.

She wanted to disturb him—emotionally, not just physically.

Turning on her heel, she walked rigidly to her bedroom and closed the door. Her eyes were hot with tears, but she didn't cry. Instead she walked to the closet and took out her nightclothes.

Lying in bed, she stared at the ceiling. Her door was shut, but the light in the hallway streamed through the narrow slit at the bottom of the door. From the living room came the whisper of papers moving against each other.

# CHAPTER NINE

OUTWARDLY THE PATTERN of their lives didn't change during the next three days, but subtly it had altered.

Cole's alarm still awakened Lacey in the mornings while he slept through its buzz.

They shared orange juice and coffee together, talking with apparently teasing friendliness. But it was a forced effort to maintain the previous week's atmosphere on both parts.

As before, Cole returned late in the evening, eating elsewhere, and spent the remainder of the time engrossed in paperwork. But there were no more physical encounters, no chance contact, because neither of them was leaving anything to chance.

For Lacey, it was like a rocket countdown. Five nights to live through before her cousin Margo returned, then four, then three. Now it was Thursday and the number was down to two.

The agony of being near him was almost over, but she was afraid of what was to come. She found it almost impossible to believe that in the space of one short week a man could mess up her mind and her life the way Cole had done.

"You stupid, impulsive little fool," she scolded herself angrily as she climbed out of her car. "He never asked you to fall in love with him, so it's your own dumb fault!''

"You're talking to yourself, Lacey. That's a bad sign," Mike teased, walking up behind her. "What are you mumbling about anyway?"

Recovering from her initial surprise, Lacey shook her head. "Nothing in particular—just the world in general."

"Did I lose a few days somewhere—is this Monday and you're on your way into the office?" He glanced ahead of them at the office building housing the construction company where they both worked.

"You haven't lost any days," she assured him, attempting a smile.

"You just couldn't stay away from the place, huh?" Mike laughed.

"Something like that," Lacey agreed.

"All joking aside, what are you doing here? You should be out soaking up the sun while you have the chance." His hazel eyes began inspecting her closely, noting the way she avoided looking directly at him and the fine tension behind her carefree expression.

"I drove over to my apartment this morning to pick up the mail and make sure everything was all right there," Lacey explained, striving to appear offhand so he wouldn't guess it was her own company she particularly wanted to avoid. "Since I was in the neighborhood and it was lunchtime, I decided to stop by and have lunch with Maryann."

"I'm afraid you're out of luck," His mouth twisted ruefully. "Maryann took her lunch break early to visit the dentist. I'd buy you lunch, but I'm just coming back myself.'' He glanced at his wristwatch. "And I have an architect due in about twenty minutes.''

"That's okay.'' Lacey shrugged, turning back to her car. "I deserve to eat alone. I should have called Maryann from my apartment instead of driving by.'' She didn't want to prolong the conversation with Mike. "See you Monday if not before, then.''

"Don't be late,'' Mike warned, waving a goodbye.

In no hurry to return to the beach house, Lacey took her time on the way back. As she passed one of the more lavish resort hotels, she studied it absently. Giving in to an impulse, a trait she had moments ago derided, she left the highway and retraced the route to the hotel.

"Go ahead and splurge,'' she insisted. "You ought to have more out of this vacation, Lacey Andrews, than a broken heart and memories.''

Parking her car in the lot, she walked into the hotel lobby, not giving herself a second chance to consider whether she should spend so much money on a simple meal. It was her vacation and she wouldn't have another for a year.

She hesitated near the lounge, trying to decide if her spree would extend to a cocktail before lunch. The thought of sitting alone at a table for two sipping a glass of wine was too depressing, and she started toward the restaurant entrance.

"Lacey!'' a male voice declared, its expression somewhere between surprise and inquiry. "My eyes didn't deceive me—it *is* you!''

Halting, Lacey turned to stare at the handsome fair-haired man striding from the lounge. Her own surprise was mingled with dismay as she recognized Monica's brother, Vic Hamilton.

"Hello, Mr. Hamilton," she greeted him coolly, hoping he would receive the message and make his greeting equally short.

He clicked his tongue in mock reproval. "Vic," he corrected smoothly, and clasped both of her unwilling hands in his. "You look as beautiful in that turquoise sundress you're wearing as you did in the pajamas of almost the same color."

There was no need for him to remind her of the circumstances surrounding their first meeting. Lacey remembered them vividly. She managed to pull one hand free, but he held the other in both of his manicured hands.

"Thank you." She smiled with artificial politeness.

"What are you doing here?" He tipped his head to the side, his smile not hiding the shrewdness in his eyes. "Don't tell me you're meeting Cole?"

"No, I'm not." Lacey had to check herself quickly to keep from snapping out the answer. "I merely stopped by for lunch."

"Alone?" Vic Hamilton lifted an inquiring brow.

"Yes, alone," Lacey answered decisively.

"I can't let you do that." His smile broadened; her answer seemed to please him. "There's nothing worse than lunching alone. Come, we'll have a drink first."

"No, thank you," she refused, trying discreetly to pull her hand free.

"If you're worried about Cole being upset because we lunched together, I wouldn't." There was something secretively amused about his look, faintly smug and knowing. "Besides, why should two people occupy two tables when they can sit together at one? If you like, we'll go dutch and you can pay for your own meal."

What was it going to take to get through to this blond god that she wasn't interested, Lacey wondered impatiently. Probably no one had ever told him no before and actually meant it.

"I. . . ." she began, but the sound of Cole's laughter coming from somewhere to her left cut off her retort.

The rich, throaty chuckle was instantly recognizable. Turning at an angle, she saw his rugged male figure, wearing a summer gray suit. As always, she experienced that little catch in her breath at the sight of him. So tanned, so vital, and so blatantly masculine, Cole seemed to fill the lobby—and Lacey's senses—with his presence.

Someone was on the receiving end of that flashing smile, full of virile charm. Resisting the pull of his magnetic attraction, Lacey forced her gaze to the person standing beside him.

Her eyes widened at the sight of the green-eyed blonde clinging to his arm. It was Monica Hamilton laughing up at Cole. Everything about the woman said this was her property; and Cole was not making any denial, token or otherwise.

"You didn't know Cole was going to be here, did you?" Vic murmured.

Lacey began to tremble violently. She was unconsciously clutching Vic's hands for support, the same ones that moments ago she had been trying to pull away from.

"No." It was a strangled sound. "I didn't know."

"Nor that he would be with my sister Monica?" Vic continued.

Completely oblivious to the ring of satisfaction in his voice, Lacey was aware only of the constricting band that seemed wrapped around her chest. The pain was so intense she thought she would die. Any second she expected her rib cage to cave in from the unbearable pressure.

. "No." Again her answer was a strangled cry.

Her hands continued to cling to him as the only solid object around. He freed one of his hands to wrap an arm around her shoulders and turn her toward the entrance to the lounge. She had the fleeting sensation of a pair of deep blue eyes narrowing on her in recognition before she was faced in another direction.

Numbed by the fierce pain, she didn't remember taking the steps that brought her to the dark corner of the lounge. The next thing she was even semiconsciously aware of was Vic gently helping her into a cushioned booth.

Imperiously he snapped his fingers for the cocktail waitress's attention and called an order, but Lacey was beyond hearing. He slid onto the seat beside her. She was trembling all over and he covered her shaking hands on the table with his own. Someone stopped at the booth, then Vic was pressing the rim of a glass against her lips.

"Drink this," he ordered, and tipped the glass.

Automatically Lacey did as she was told, coughing and choking as the liquor burned a path down her throat. Once again she could feel, but she wasn't certain that she was grateful for that. Seeing Cole like that, looking so happy with Monica, left her with the feeling that she had been betrayed and used.

"Cole didn't mention to you that he's been seeing Monica, did he?" Vic observed.

Pain stabbed through her at his suggestion that this wasn't the first time. She gave him a stricken look, then lowered her head, shaking it briefly.

"No, he didn't," she admitted.

"Haven't you wondered where he's been having his evening meals?" Vic chided in a tone that reproved her blindness.

"No, I. . . ." Lacey pressed a trembling hand over her eyes. It had never occurred to her to set the record straight that she and Cole were not living together in the intimate sense of the phrase. "I thought he was stopping at a restaurant somewhere."

"He's spent the last three evenings at our house, dining with Monica," he informed her.

"I see," Lacey murmured.

She saw that she had been a fool to hold out any hope where Cole was concerned. The hand covering hers tightened protectively, squeezing a warning an instant before a tall figure blocked the light. Lacey guessed it was Cole before he spoke, her nerves sharpening to a razor edge.

"What are you doing here, Lacey?" His voice was low and tautly controlled.

Lowering her hand from her face, she looked up at him, her eyes bright with pain. The hard angles and planes of his features were set in expressionless lines, yet she sensed his anger simmering just below the surface.

From somewhere she found the strength to challenge him. He had no right to an explanation for her presence in this hotel.

"What most people do at a place like this," she retorted, her tone brittle. "I'm having a drink before lunch."

"Yes, Lacey took pity on me being alone and agreed to join me," volunteered Vic, and Lacey didn't deny the lie.

The muscles along Cole's jawline tightened noticeably as he flashed an accusing look at Lacey. Monica appeared at his elbow, eyeing Lacey for a brief second before smiling possessively at Cole.

"Darling, they're holding our table," she reminded him huskily.

Distracted, Cole glanced down at her. He hesitated for a fraction of a second, then his gaze pinned Lacey again, sharp and metallic blue.

"Would you join us?" he requested stiffly.

"No," she refused, lowering her pain-filled gaze to the liquor glass on the table.

Beside her, Vic shrugged. "The lady says no, Cole. And I certainly don't have any reason to try to change her mind."

"Our table," Monica prodded.

Out of her side vision, Lacey saw Cole abruptly pivot away from the booth. The rigidity of controlled anger was in his carriage as he walked from the lounge with Monica on his arm. Pain shuddered through Lacey, relief mixed with a wounding ache.

"You're in love with him, aren't you?" Vic's statement was coated with sardonic mockery.

Pale and shaken, Lacey knew she couldn't escape the truth, so she nodded a silent admission. There was a terrible unreality to the situation, as if none of it was really happening.

"You poor kid." But he sounded more amused than sorry for her. "You thought you had a chance against Monica. If you'd asked me, I could have told you it was inevitable that Cole would end up with her."

"Really?" Tears seemed to be frozen on her lashes. She flicked them away with her finger, refusing to break down, but more returned to hang like liquid icicles. She breathed in deeply, sniffling a little, but obtaining some control.

"Monica has too many things going for her," Vic told her. "Besides, Cole is just the kind of man she needs. He would have been hers two years ago if she hadn't started ordering him around and throwing childish tantrums when he wouldn't do what she wanted. Theirs has been an on-again-off-again affair ever since. You have met Cole in one of the off-again stages."

"Yes, probably," Lacey agreed tightly, not about to explain their meeting now.

"To be perfectly frank, I'm all in favor of the marriage," he went on. "With Cole for a brother-in-law, I know my father will get off my back. I haven't any business sense and I don't want anything to do with the family operations."

He slid an arm around her shoulders again. At first Lacey accepted its comfort. "I'm not cut out for the business world, and Cole is. I'm much better at consoling beautiful women like you, Lacey."

She stiffened at his words. "If you're the consolation

prize for losing Cole, Mr. Hamilton, I'm not interested," she declared, and removed his arm from around her shoulders. "Would you please let me out of this booth?" she requested curtly.

Vic Hamilton was not interested in consoling her, only in taking advantage of her weakness at the moment. To remain in his company would simply remind her that Cole was with Monica. At long last she realized what a fool she had made of herself by falling in love with Cole. There was no need to make a bigger fool of herself.

"Where are you going?" He appeared incredulous that she was actually rejecting him.

"I'm leaving, and 'where' is my business," she retorted.

"You don't really mean it," Vic persisted.

"I do. So if you don't want me to create a scene, you will move."

He gave her an ugly smile. "You'll be sorry for this some day. Once a girl says no to me, it's the last time she's ever asked," he threatened.

"No, Mr. Hamilton. No, no, I don't want you ever," Lacey repeated, enunciating each word.

White with anger, he slid out of the booth. "You're nothing but a stupid little secretary," he jeered. "I don't know why I bothered with you."

His spiteful words bounced off her, not leaving any marks, as she swept past him to the lobby. When she stepped outside into the sun, the tears on her lashes streamed down her cheeks.

Once she was in her car, instinct took over, making all the right turns to take her to the beach house. She drove

the last two miles in a sea of tears that blinded her to the
point that she could barely make out the road.

Bolting into the house, she stumbled up the stairs to
sink into the nearest chair, drowning in waves of despair
and self-pity. Outside a car engine roared angrily into
the driveway, brakes squealing it to a halt short of the
garage door. The reverberation of a car door being
slammed echoed into the house.

A sixth sense warned Lacey it was Cole. She quickly
wiped the tears from her face and was blowing her nose
as he slammed more doors on his way into the house,
climbing the stairs two at a time.

His anger was no longer suppressed, but raging freely
in his every line. But Lacey was beyond being intimi-
dated by his anger; he had already hurt her too deeply
for that. She met the blue storm clouds of his gaze
without flinching.

"It's a little early for you to be here, isn't it?" she
suggested stiffly.

"You know damned well why I'm here!" His voice
rolled like thunder across the room and Cole quickly
followed it. His hands were clenched in fists at his side,
muscles leaping along his jaw. "I want to know what
you were doing at that hotel with Hamilton."

Lacey tilted her chin defiantly, pain hammering at her
throat. "It's no concern of yours what I was doing at
the hotel or with whom!"

If she had had any doubts about that statement, they
had faded into nothing when she had seen him with
Monica. She started to pivot away from him, but his
fingers closed in an iron grip around her forearm to spin
her back.

"When I ask a question, I want an answer," he growled savagely. "What were you doing at the hotel?"

"You're hurting my arm," she pointed out curtly. His punishing grip began to cut off the circulation, making her hand and wrist throb.

"A lot more is going to hurt if you don't give me a straight answer," he warned, not relaxing his hold a fraction.

"I certainly didn't go because I thought you would be there." Lacey choked out the answer, fighting the tears that were once again stinging her eyes.

"But you arranged to meet Vic Hamilton there, didn't you?" Cole accused.

"Yes, I met him there. Is that what you wanted to hear?" she cried in challenge.

He released her arm abruptly as if she had suddenly become contaminated. With fires still raging in his eyes, he looked away in angry exasperation. He let his gaze slice back to her, dissecting her into little pieces.

"I knew it was only a matter of time before Vic made a play for you, but I thought you were smart enough to know what a philanderer he is," he said with contempt. "But the combination of money and looks was too much for you, wasn't it?" He didn't wait for an answer. "How many other times have you met him before to-day?"

Lacey was gently massaging her arm where he had gripped her so roughly. There would be bruises in the morning where his fingers had dug into her flesh.

"It isn't any concern of yours," she declared tightly, countering with, "I've never asked you how many times you've seen Monica."

"Monica has no part in this, so just leave her out of it!" he snapped.

"Gladly!"

Lacey stalked out of the living room onto the balcony. Her fingers curled into the railing, her nails digging into the smooth painted surface. Waves of pain racked her system, leaving her shaken and trembling.

She was angry with herself because she was letting Cole tear up her emotions further when the damage he had already done was beyond repair. She used that anger as a protective shield against him when he followed her onto the balcony.

"Lacey, I want you to stay away from Vic Hamilton," he ordered. His anger was held in check by a very tight rein, capable of snapping at the slightest provocation.

"I'll do as I please where Vic Hamilton or anyone else is concerned," Lacey retorted in a low, trembling voice that was fierce in her attempt to establish an independence. "Not you, nor any man, has the right to tell me whom I may see!"

The fragile reins of his temper snapped. Her shoulders were seized and roughly shaken as if she were a rag doll. The pain ripping through her body made her as weak and limp as one.

"Do I have to shake some sense into you?" he demanded gruffly.

"I think you've already tried." Her laugh was brittle, her already rattled senses in worse shape than before.

"Then listen to me and stay away from him," he declared, gritting his teeth in determination.

With a supreme effort, Lacey pushed and twisted out

of his hold. "I don't have to listen to you!" she cried angrily, her voice ringing with the pulsing hurt inside, her nerves raw. "You don't have any right to tell me what to do or not to do! I don't tell you who you can have for friends, and you're not going to tell me!"

His smoldering gaze flashed past her for an instant. "You don't have to shout, Lacey," he reproved in a low, sharp tone.

Automatically she glanced over her shoulder, an unconscious reaction to discover what had distracted his attention. A woman wearing a sunbonnet was on the beach near the tideline. Lacey recognized her instantly. It was the Mrs. Carlyle, who regularly searched the beach for seashells, and she was staring toward the house, the ocean air undoubtedly carrying their angry voices to her.

"I will shout if I want to." But Lacey did lower her volume. "And if you don't like it, you can leave!"

"We've been through that before," Cole retorted.

"Yes, we have." Her chin quivered traitorously. "And you'll be glad to learn that you've finally won that argument. I'm leaving!"

Cole frowned, his gaze narrowing in surprise at her announcement. Lacey didn't wait to hear his response, but darted past him into the house, not slowing up until she had reached her bedroom. The decision had been made on impulse, but she knew it was the only recourse left open to her.

Gulping back sobs, she dragged her suitcases from the closet and tossed them onto the bed. She began gathering her clothes and stuffing them carelessly into the open bags, jamming them together with no thought to orderliness. She hesitated for a split second when Cole appeared in the doorway before continuing her hurried packing.

A muscle was working convulsively along his jaw. His mouth was a grim line, but there was regret flickering in the hard blue steel of his gaze.

"Lacey, I—" he began tautly.

"There's nothing left to say," she interrupted briskly, aware of his tall muscular figure filling the door frame. "I have three full days of my vacation left and I'm not going to let you ruin those for me."

Impatiently he burst out, "Dammit, Lacey, I'm not trying to ruin anything for you. I—"

"You've certainly done a first-rate job for someone who wasn't trying!" She slammed a handful of clothes into one of the cases, her voice growing thick with suppressed emotion.

"You don't understand," Cole muttered.

"Isn't it time you were going back to your office?" challenged Lacey, scooping a handful of cosmetics from the dresser and dumping them into their small case.

"Yes, it is, but first—"

She turned on him roundly, trembling from the mental anguish his presence induced. "I'm leaving! The house is yours! Isn't that what you want?"

His expression hardened, his mouth compressed into a thin line. "Yes," he snapped after a second's hesitation. "That is exactly what I want!"

In the next instant the doorway was empty. Heavy, angry strides were carrying him down the hallway. Lacey resumed her packing in a frenzied need for activity, faltering briefly when she heard the door slam below.

AN HOUR AND A HALF later, she was carrying the last of her belongings into her own apartment. Setting the bag on the floor, she collapsed into one of the chairs, burying her face in her hands.

She didn't cry; there didn't seem to be any tears inside her. She was just a big empty ache. Vital parts had been removed and she knew she would never function quite the same again.

The telephone rang. It seemed an eternity since she had heard the sound. She stared at it blankly for several rings before pushing herself out of the chair to answer it.

"Hello," she said in a tired and dispirited voice.

"Lacey?"

It was Cole. The sound of his voice seemed to slash at her heart like a knife. Lacey hung up the phone to stop the piercing hurt.

Within minutes it was ringing again. She had made up her mind not to answer it when her hand picked up the receiver of its own volition and carried it to her ear.

"Don't hang up, Lacey." The remnants of his temper were evident in his irritated tone. "I'm at my office, so I don't have time to argue. We're going to get together tonight so we can talk this thing out. I'll be free around eight-thirty...."

After he had dined with Monica, Lacey realized. "Leave me alone!" she begged angrily. "Get out of my life and stay out of it! I don't want to see or hear from you again—ever!"

She slammed the receiver down, breaking the connection, but Cole was as stubborn as she was. He would call back. Trembling, Lacey picked up the telephone again, hesitated, then dialed a number.

When it was answered, she said, "Jane? This is Lacey. May I speak to Maryann?"

"Sure," was the reply. "How is your vacation?"

"Fine," Lacey lied, and her call was switched through. "Hello, Maryann?"

"Hi, Lacey," was the cheerful response. "Mike told me you stopped this noon for lunch. I only wish I'd known you were coming—it would have given me a perfect excuse to cancel my dental appointment."

"I should have called you in the morning, but I didn't think of it," Lacey replied absently.

"How are you enjoying the sun and the sand and the surf?"

"That's what I'm calling about," she began hesitantly. "I'm not at the beach house. I've moved out."

"Good heavens, what happened?" Maryann asked with instant concern.

"It's a long story." Her friend already knew part of it from the visit Lacey had made the previous Friday night. "I was wondering if I could sleep on your couch for a few nights."

"Of course," was the puzzled reply, "but I thought you were going to Richmond to visit your parents this weekend after Margo came back."

"I was, but I've changed my mind."

The thought of explaining to her parents all that had happened was too daunting, and Lacey knew she would never be able to keep it from them. They were too close. And she couldn't stay in her apartment. Cole would keep phoning and possibly even come over.

"What happened, Lacey? Did—"

"I'll tell you all about it tonight," she promised. "What time will you be getting off work?"

"I shouldn't have any trouble leaving by five, but I have to stop at the bank and the store." Maryann paused. "Why don't you stop by the office and I'll give you the key to my apartment? That way you won't have to wait for me," she suggested.

"Thanks." Lacey swallowed, her throat suddenly constricting.

"Oh, I have a motive," her friend laughed. "If I have to wait until tonight to find out what happened, I'll be insane with curiosity. When you stop by, you can give me an outline at least."

# CHAPTER TEN

RETURNING TO WORK on Monday morning, Lacey hoped her job would take her mind off the dead ache of her heart. So far that hope hadn't shown much promise. She had difficulty concentrating. Typing a letter was proving to be an impossible task as her fingers constantly hit the wrong keys.

"You look as if you could use some coffee. Shall I pour you a cup?" Mike offered, pausing beside her desk to reach for her coffee mug.

"Please," Lacey sighed, then bent over her typewriter to erase her latest error.

Mike filled her cup as well as his own and set it back on her desk. "It's only ten o'clock in the morning and you look bushed. I think that's a symptom of what's known as the first-day-back-from-vacation malady," he teased as his hazel gaze made an assessing sweep of her.

"Probably," she agreed, and removed the corrected letter from the typewriter carriage to add it to the stack on her desk. "Here are the letters you wanted out this morning."

"Mmm, good," said Mike between sips of his coffee. He gathered up the pile of letters and walked to the connecting door to his private office. He paused in the doorway. "It's good to have you back, Lacey."

"Thanks." It was a weary smile that accompanied her reply, etched with strain.

As he closed the door behind him, she rested her elbows on the desk top. Her shoulders slumped as if the weight of keeping up the appearance that she was her normal self had become too heavy to maintain when no one was around to see.

With the tips of her fingers she rubbed the throbbing pressure point between her eyebrows. She blinked at the tears that unexpectedly sprang into her eyes.

The door to the main office area opened and she straightened to an erect posture. The forced smile of polite greeting she had affixed to her lips drooped as Cole walked into the office.

He looked haggard and worn, but there was a relentlessly unyielding set to his jaw. It seemed to match the determined glitter in his indigo blue eyes.

Recovering from her initial shock, Lacey reached for the phone, ringing the interoffice line to Mike. "Cole Whitfield is here to see you, Mike," she said the minute that he answered her buzz.

"What?" His stunned reaction indicated that he had not expected Cole.

Lacey's pulse skyrocketed in alarm. "I'll. . . ."

Cole reached over her desk and pushed the button to break the connection. "I'm not here to see Bowman," he stated. "It's you I want to talk to, Lacey."

Hastily she replaced the receiver and gathered the miscellaneous folders and papers from the filing basket. She rose quickly from her chair to walk to the filing cabinet, wanting distance between herself and Cole.

"Did Margo and Bob get back safely?" She tried to

make the question sound nonchalant, pretending an indifference to his presence as she pulled open a file drawer.

Cole was right behind her to push the drawer shut. Her heart began leaping like a jumping bean. Raw, aching nerves were crying out for relief.

"As a matter of fact, they did," he said tersely. "But that's not why I'm here and you know it."

The connecting office door opened and Mike stepped out, frowning bewilderedly at Cole. "I'm sorry about the confusion, Cole, but Lacey's replacement must have forgotten to leave a message that you were coming this morning. What was it you wanted to talk to me about?"

Cole flashed an impatient look at him, annoyed by the interruption. "It isn't you I'm here to see," he repeated. "I want a few words with Lacey, if you don't mind."

·The latter phrase was merely a polite gesture. Lacey had the impression Cole would stay whether Mike gave his permission or not.

"We have nothing to discuss," she told him stiffly, and brushed past him to return to her desk.

"That's where you're wrong," Cole stated flatly. "We have a great deal to discuss."

"This sounds private," Mike muttered, and retreated behind his office door.

Lacey turned to call him back and came face to face with Cole. All her senses were heightened by his closeness; she was quivering in reaction to his forceful presence.

"Why don't you go away and leave me alone?" she demanded hoarsely. "Can't you see I'm working?"

"You chose the time and place. I didn't," Cole informed her. "You knew I wanted to speak to you. I've been trying all weekend to get hold of you, but you've been hiding somewhere."

"I was not hiding!" she lied, and angrily shoved the papers back into the filing basket.

"Oh?" A dark brow was raised in mocking skepticism. "What do you call it?"

"Enjoying what remained of my vacation," Lacey retorted, and started to walk away from him again.

His hand caught at the soft flesh of her upper arm to stop her. "Will you stand still?" he demanded in an exasperated breath.

His touch burned through her like a branding iron and Lacey reacted as violently as if it were, trying to wrench her arm out of his grip. Cole merely tightened his hold.

"Let me go!" she hissed, pathetically vulnerable to his touch.

Desperate, she grabbed for the first item on her desk top that could be used as a weapon. It turned out to be the stapler. She raised it to strike him, but Cole captured her wrist before she could even begin the swing.

"This is where I came in, isn't it?" The grim line of his mouth twisted wryly as she was pulled close by her struggles. "Only the other time you were trying to bash my head in with a poker."

"I hate you, Cole Whitfield!" Her voice was breaking. "You are the rudest, most arrogant—"

"You said something similar to that before, too." He pried the stapler free from the death-grip of her fingers and replaced it on the desk top. "Now, do you think we can sit down and talk this out like two civilized human beings?''

Averting her head from the tantalizing nearness of his well-formed mouth, she nodded reluctantly. "Yes."

"Sit down." Cole more or less pushed her into her chair and drew a second for himself opposite hers.

"I still don't see that we have anything to talk about," she insisted stubbornly, her pulse behaving not quite as erratically as it had seconds ago in his arms.

"For starters—" the direct blue eyes studied her closely "—why didn't you tell me that you didn't go to the hotel to meet Vic Hamilton?"

"You weren't in any mood to listen to me and I didn't see why I should explain." After the defensive answer, she hesitated and asked, "How did you find out?"

"From Vic, after a little prompting," Cole answered with a half smile. "Luckily for him, he was too concerned about having his handsome face messed up, so it took only a few threats. As angry as I was, I would have beaten the truth out of him."

"It wasn't any of your business," Lacey muttered, looking away. She refused to read any implication into his personal involvement in her affairs.

"Wasn't it?" he asked quietly, his low voice rolling over her skin.

The interoffice line buzzed and she reached for the phone, grateful for the interruption. But Cole took the receiver out of her hand.

"Hold all the calls. Don't put any more through," he ordered and hung up.

"You can't do that," Lacey protested in astonishment.

"That's funny—I thought I just did," he countered with a laughing glint in his eye.

"You know what I mean," she retorted impatiently.

"But do you know what I mean?" His voice was wistfully soft and enigmatic.

Its tug on her heartstrings was more than she could bear. Agitatedly she rose from her chair, her hands clasped tightly in front of her.

"There isn't any point to this conversation," she insisted. "Everything has been said. Our little interlude, affair, whatever you want to call it, is over. You are free to go your way and I'm free to go mine."

"Is that the way you want it?" Cole sounded skeptical.

Lacey knew she had to convince him somehow that it was what she wanted, even though she knew with all her heart that it wasn't.

"Yes, that is the way I want it," she repeated stiffly. "So I don't see what there is for us to discuss."

In a fluid move, Cole was behind her, his hands settling lightly on her shoulders to turn her to face him. Lacey could find no strength to resist his undemanding touch.

"The point to this conversation is that I miss you," he said quietly. He ran his gaze over her face, and she caught her breath at the fires smoldering in his eyes. "It's been pure and simple misery since you left. You're not there in the mornings anymore to wake me up when I sleep through the alarm. No coffee, no orange juice made. I never minded before coming home to an empty house, but I do now after having you there to greet me. And in the evenings, I can't get any work done without you sitting quietly in a nearby chair."

"You make me sound as if I've become a habit." There was a painful lump in her throat, choking her.

"A very pleasurable habit that I don't want to give up," Cole responded, stroking a hand over her cheek into the silken brown of her hair.

"What are you suggesting, Cole?" Tears were misting her eyes when she met his look, doubt stealing pleasure from his words. "That we should resume our arrangement of living together, throwing out the ground rules?"

"And if I said yes, what would you say?" That glowing look in his eyes was tugging at her heart.

Lacey struggled with her pride. "I would say, thanks but no thanks. I'm not interested in taking on a lover at the present time." Just for a moment she weakened to ask, "That is what you're suggesting, isn't it?"

"In a sense, yes." His slow smile was disarming. "I want to marry you, Lacey. I want you to be my wife."

"Oh!" The tiny word escaped in an indrawn breath of surprise as she melted slightly against him. "Are you serious? What about Monica?"

"Monica?" A curious frown creased his forehead. "Why should she have anything to do with it?"

"I don't know." She was confused and uncertain about the conclusion she had previously drawn. "You dined with her all last week, didn't you?"

"At her parents' home, yes, and she was at the table, but it was her father I was meeting, not Monica," Cole explained in amusement. "Who told you I was there? Vic, I suppose."

"Yes," Lacey nodded, and sighed when his arm tightened around her waist. "He said that ever since you broke your engagement with Monica, you had continued to go on seeing her."

"And you believed him," he concluded.

"I believed him. You were there at the hotel with her, having lunch. He said your relationship with her had been an on-again, off-again affair and that I had met you during one of the off-again times. It seemed logical," Lacey said, trying to defend the erroneous conclusion she had reached.

"I should have known he would make mischief of some sort," he concluded, bending his head to brush his mouth over the warmth of her skin, teasingly near her lips. Her lashes fluttered in tempo with her heart. "I have business dealings with Carter Hamilton, her father. That's the only reason I was there."

Her hands slipped nearer to the collar of his shirt. "I didn't know," she whispered. "I thought—at the hotel, you looked so happy with her. Not like the other time when you were...."

"Rude, is that the word you're looking for?" Cole finished, mockingly. "That Sunday at the beach house, Monica arrived uninvited. I saw no reason to be polite to a woman who wasn't welcome in my home. And if you had the impression I was happy to be with her at the hotel, I'm a better actor than I realized. Regardless of how it looked, I was merely being polite to the daughter of a business associate, even if she's an ugly old crow."

"Monica's beautiful," Lacey protested.

"That, my love, is in the eye of the beholder," he corrected, drawing his head back to look at her. "When are you going to stop talking so I can kiss you?"

"Now."

Her hands slid around his neck as she raised herself on tiptoes to meet his descending mouth. Joy spilled over, lighting every corner of her world.

The taste of his mouth possessively covering hers was like a sweet wine that went to her head, and Lacey felt drunk with the rapture of love returned. When the kiss ended on a reluctant note, she rested her head on his shoulder, deliriously happy in a quiet kind of way.

"You haven't said you'll marry me yet." His voice was a husky tremor.

"Haven't I?" she returned with faint surprise. Tipping her head back, she smiled at his soberly rapt expression. "I will."

"Do you have any objection to a quick elopement?"

"None." She shook her head. She lifted a hand to let her fingertips trace the forceful line of his jaw. "Why did you let me leave last Thursday? You acted as if you were glad to see me go."

"I was." He caught her hand, lightly kissing the tips of her fingers. "It was sheer torture lying in bed at nights with you in the next room. If you'd stayed those last two nights, I knew I would throw those stupid ground rules out the window. When you decided to leave, I never expected you'd disappear. It turned out to be worse not knowing where you were or who you were with."

"I stayed at a girl friend's," Lacey said in answer to his unspoken question.

"While I went quietly out of my mind," Cole added wryly.

"I'm sorry," she whispered.

"You should be," he declared with mock gruffness.

"I wasn't having an easy time of it, either, this weekend," Lacey reminded him. "I kept imagining you with Monica and wondering when I would read about your engagement in the newspapers."

"There has never been any reason for you to be jealous of Monica," Cole assured her.

"I know that...now." But she hoped she would never have to live through another weekend like that again.

The remembered pain must have been reflected in her eyes, because Cole's dark gaze became suddenly very intense. "Never forget that I love you, Lacey." He kissed her hard and fiercely, as if to drive out the painful memory so there would be room only for his love.

The interoffice door opened and Mike walked through, halting at the sight of the embracing pair. "Sorry. It was so quiet out here I thought you'd gone, Whitfield," he apologized, and started to retreat.

"There's no need to leave, Mike," said Cole. "Lacey and I were just going."

"What?" Mike frowned and Lacey stared at Cole in confusion and surprise.

"I'll have someone over to replace her in half an hour," Cole continued. "She's going to have a lot to do in the next few days. And after we're married, if she wants to be anyone's secretary, I'd rather have her be mine."

"But...." Lacey didn't know what protest she was about to make since she didn't really object to Cole's plan.

"In the meantime," Cole interrupted, "there's something I want to show her."

She forgot all about Mike and how he would get along without a secretary.

"What?" Her curiosity was aroused.

"Get your purse and I'll show you." He smiled mysteriously.

"Congratulations," Mike offered as Cole hurried Lacey out the door.

As Cole was helping her into his car, Lacey repeated her question, "What are you going to show me?"

"You'll see," was all he would say.

"Give me a hint at least," she persisted.

But his only response was an enigmatic smile as he pulled out of the parking lot into the street.

Within a short time, she realized they were driving toward Virginia Beach, crossing the Chesapeake Bay bridge-tunnel into Norfolk. When they turned onto a side road she recognized, she became thoroughly confused. It led to her cousin Margo's house.

"Why are we going to the beach house?" She frowned.

Cole reached for her hand and held it warmly in his. "Patience."

At the house, he parked the car in the driveway and turned to face her, smiling. "Would the future Mrs. Whitfield like to see her new home?"

"What?" She gave him an incredulous look and he chuckled softly.

"When Margo and Bob came back from their cruise, he told me that they were moving to Florida near his parents as soon as he could make all the arrangements here." He reached in his pocket and handed her a key. "I bought the house for us. After all the frustrating nights I'd spent here with you, I decided it was fitting that this should be our home where I can spend a million satisfying evenings with you."

"You've bought it?" Lacey stared at the key in the palm of her hand, not certain that she had really understood him.

"You did like the house, didn't you?" Cole tipped his head to the side, studying her closely, a ring of uncertainty in his voice.

"I love the house!" she declared vigorously. "I just can't believe it's really mine—ours," she corrected herself quickly.

"Believe it, honey."

A sound, somewhere between a laugh and a cry, came from her throat as she threw her arms around his neck, happiness and love bubbling from her like an eternal fountain. Cole removed the need to express herself with words. Deeds were much more enjoyable.

Her arms were locked around Cole's neck when he finally lifted his mouth from her lips. "Would it be improper to prematurely carry my bride over the threshold?"

"Why worry about whether it's proper or not?" Lacey questioned in an amused voice. "You've already carried me into your bedroom."

"So I have." He grinned and swept her up into the cradle of his arms.

The key to the front door was still clutched in her fingers. Lacey was certain Cole was going to drop her before she was able to insert it in the lock and open the door. Laughing, he carried her into the house and up the stairs, kissing her soundly as he set her on her feet. Lacey glanced around, catching back the sob in her throat.

"What's the matter?" Cole frowned curiously.

"I'm afraid this is all a dream and I'm going to wake up," she murmured. He pinched her arm. "Ouch!"

"It isn't a dream. I'm still here and you still have the key to our house in your hand," he told her, his eyes crinkling at the corners.

"I can't believe it," Lacey insisted with a shake of her head, adding a quick, "but don't pinch me again. That hurt."

"I promise not to damage the merchandise until I'm sure it's totally mine. Which reminds me, when we leave here, we'll drive to Richmond. Your parents might like to meet me before I marry their daughter."

"Good heavens!" she declared as she realized the truth of his words. "My parents have never even heard of you. I haven't written them or talked to them on the phone since I met you. What will they think?"

"They'll think that I swept you off your feet, the way every romantic lover should," he mocked.

She laughed. "Just wait until I tell Maryann."

"Who is Maryann?"

"My friend. My very best friend." Lacey made the definition a little more emphatic.

"The same one you stayed with this weekend?" Cole asked.

"Yes, the very same."

"I suppose she's the one you'll run to whenever we have an argument."

"More than likely," Lacey retorted.

"I want her name, address and telephone number so I'll know where to find you the next time you storm out of the house."

"Do you think there will be a next time?" She tipped her head to the side, finding it difficult to imagine that she could ever get that angry with him again.

"Probably," Cole sighed. "We're both pretty stubborn."

"You are more stubborn than I am," Lacey reminded him.

"You see?" He tweaked the tip of her nose. "You're already trying to start an argument."

"It seems to me a smart fellow like you might be able to figure out how to shut me up." Her brown eyes were bright with silent invitation.

"It will be very enjoyable trying," he declared before seeking her lips.

COLE WADED from the water, a bronze-skinned sea god emerging from the ocean, and love tingled over Lacey's flesh at the sight of him walking toward her, the flashing white of his smile lighting her life.

An interlocking diamond solitaire ring and gold wedding band was on the third finger of her left hand, proof that she really was his wife. Yet often in the past few days, Lacey had been overcome with the urge to pinch herself to be reassured it wasn't just a beautiful dream. Every time she looked at Cole, touched him, she fell in love with him all over again.

Reaching her side, he dropped to his knees on the sand, droplets of salt water clinging to him. For a minute he simply studied her, stretched on the sand in her metallic blue gray swimsuit.

Instantly every nerve was alert, her senses quivering at the disturbing ardor in his look. He reached for her hand, pulling her into a sitting position, then kissing her with familiar ease.

"Happy?" he murmured, raking his fingers through her short brown hair and cupping the back of her head in his hand.

"Heavenly so, if there is such a thing," Lacey answered softly, a delicious warmth spreading through her limbs.

"Even though we have to set the alarm to get up in the morning?" Cole reminded her wryly.

"Are you dreading breaking in your new secretary?" she teased.

"I don't know." The creases along the corners of his mouth deepened attractively. "I've certainly enjoyed breaking in my new wife these past few days."

"Have you?" Her lips parted, inviting his kiss.

His dark blue gaze flicked to them for a tantalizing second, a fire smoldering to life in his eyes. Then he was straightening, pulling her to her feet along with him. The kiss he gave her held a promise of more to come in a more private place than the beach.

When he turned toward the house, an arm was curved around Lacey's waist to tuck her close to his side. A woman was walking to their right, intent upon the sand at her feet. The old-fashioned sunbonnet on her head instantly identified the woman to Cole and Lacey. He stopped.

"Good afternoon, Mrs. Carlyle," he greeted her.

The woman glanced up, momentarily surprised. "Good afternoon." Her gaze took in the affectionate attitude of the pair. "I see the two of you here made up after your little spat." Despite the friendliness in her remark, there was evidence of disapproval in the tightness of her smile.

"We did," Cole admitted, adding with a dancing light in his eye, "And I took your advice, too." He held up Lacey's left hand, showing off the gold band encircling her ring finger. "I made an honest woman of her."

Immediately the woman's smile turned into a radiant beam. "I'm delighted for both of you, really I am. As much in love as the two of you are, you won't be sorry," she insisted.

"No, we won't be a bit sorry," Cole agreed, and smiled down at Lacey's upturned face.

# ROMANCE IS A YEARLONG EVENT!

Celebrate the most romantic day of the year with MY VALENTINE! (February)

CRYSTAL CREEK
When you come for a visit Texas-style, you won't want to leave! (March)

Celebrate the joy, excitement and adjustment that comes with being JUST MARRIED! (April)

Go back in time and discover the West as it was meant to be . . . UNTAMED—Maverick Hearts! (July)

LINGERING SHADOWS
*New York Times* bestselling author Penny Jordan brings you her latest blockbuster. Don't miss it! (August)

BACK BY POPULAR DEMAND!!!
Calloway Corners, involving stories of four sisters coping with family, business and romance! (September)

FRIENDS, FAMILIES, LOVERS
Join us for these heartwarming love stories that evoke memories of family and friends. (October)

Capture the magic and romance of Christmas past with HARLEQUIN HISTORICAL CHRISTMAS STORIES! (November)

## WATCH FOR FURTHER DETAILS IN ALL HARLEQUIN BOOKS!

CALEND

# WELCOME TO

### The quintessential small town,
### where everyone knows everybody else!

Each book set in Tyler is a self-contained love story; together,
the twelve novels stitch the fabric of the community.

### "Scintillating romance!"
### "Immensely appealing characters...wonderful intensity and
### humor."
### *Romantic Times*

Join your friends in Tyler for the eleventh book,
COURTHOUSE STEPS by Ginger Chambers, available in January.

*Was Margaret's husband responsible for her murder?*
*What memories come flooding back to Alyssa?*

### GREAT READING...GREAT SAVINGS...AND A
### FABULOUS FREE GIFT!

With Tyler you can receive a fabulous gift, ABSOLUTELY FREE,
by collecting proofs-of-purchase found in each Tyler book.
And use our special Tyler coupons to save on your next
TYLER book purchase.

---

## COME FOR A VISIT—TEXAS-STYLE!

**Where do you find hot Texas nights, smooth Texas charm and dangerously sexy cowboys? CRYSTAL CREEK!**

This March, join us for a year in Crystal Creek...where power and influence live in the land, and in the hands of one family determined to nourish old Texas fortunes and to forge new Texas futures.

CRYSTAL CREEK reverberates with the exciting rhythm of Texas. Each story features the rugged individuals who live and love in the Lone Star State. And each one ends with the same invitation...

### Y'ALL COME BACK...REAL SOON!

Watch for this exciting saga of a unique Texas family in March, wherever Harlequin Books are sold.

CC-G

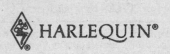